# PRAISE FOR WHEN MORNING COMES

"This timely reminder of the power and passion of young people contextualizes current student protests by honoring those of the past."
—*Kirkus Reviews* (starred review)

"Raina's story powerfully demonstrates the high stakes of the teenagers' choices while maintaining a bracing pace that builds steady tension."
—*Publisher's Weekly* (starred review)

"Raina's novel provides a riveting and candid depiction of life in South Africa at the cusp of an uprising which would eventually dismantle apartheid. But it is also a story of complicated friendships, a doomed love affair and the surprising strength and resilience of four young people living in impossible times."—*Canadian Children's Book News*

"*When Morning Comes* . . . has an in-the-moment, documentary feel that puts historical realism and authenticity first."—*The Globe and Mail*

"Readers . . . will recognize parallel themes from youth involvement in the American civil rights movement (and) historical fiction fans will find common ground here with teens who favor dramatic thrillers."
—*Bulletin of the Center for Children's Books*

"This novel presents an excellent starting point to inspire curiosity, and serves as a bold and dignified testament to a struggle that shouldn't be forgotten."—*Quill and Quire*

"An eye-opening view of a rarely covered time and place in YA literature, this title offers rich opportunities for discussion and classroom sharing."—*The School Library Journal*

"Class and race intersect at a pivotal moment in history as the compelling characters—a wide cross section of South Africans— offer their stories, and a day in the life of a country in crisis comes into focus."—*Booklist*

"(This) novel itself is a far stronger exposition of the students' anger and power than any historical commentary could be." *Resource Links*

"At its best, historical fiction allows us to feel as if we are living through something we have only read about. That is especially true in the case of *When Morning Comes*."—*The Montreal Gazette*

# WHEN MORNING COMES

## ARUSHI RAINA

**TRADEWIND BOOKS**
VANCOUVER • LONDON

Published in Canada and the UK in 2016
Published in the USA in 2017

Text © 2016 by Arushi Raina
Cover illustration © 2016 by Elisa Gutiérrez
Cover design by Elisa Gutiérrez
Book design by Jacqueline Wang

The paper is 100% post-consumer recycled and processed chlorine and acid-free.

Printed in Canada

2 4 6 8 10 9 7 5

Cataloguing-in-Publication Data for this book
is available from The British Library.

Library and Archives Canada Cataloguing in Publication

Raina, Arushi, author
  When morning comes / Arushi Raina.

ISBN 978-1-896580-69-2 (hardback).--
ISBN 978-1-926890-14-2 (paperback)

  I. Title.

PS8635.A427W44 2016      jC813'.6      C2016-901027-9

*Tradewind Books thanks the Governments of Canada and British Columbia for
the financial support they have extended through the Canada Book Fund, Livres
Canada Books, the Canada Council for the Arts, the British Columbia Arts
Council and the British Columbia Book Publishing Tax Credit program.*

Canada Council
for the Arts

Conseil des Arts
du Canada

BRITISH COLUMBIA
ARTS COUNCIL
Supported by the Province of British Columbia

LIVRES CANADA BOOKS

*The publisher wishes to thank Ayushi Nayak and Olga Lenczewska for their editorial help with this book.*

# ACKNOWLEDGEMENTS

Even imagined uprisings rely on many voices. Thanks to Tevin Radebe for his handy advice on Zulu and Xhosa. To Vis Naidoo—a pamphleteer in his time. To John Wulz for helping Meena dissect and examine bodies for causes of death.

Thanks to my publishers, Mike and Carol, for believing in this book when it most mattered, for their passionate support for the stories less told. And to Sue Ann for caring so deeply for Meena, Jack, Zanele—even Thabo. To Christianne, for the fierce loyalty, wisdom and compassion she brings to all things. Thanks to Cecil Hershler for his encouragement.

To Don Foster for teaching me to use words with care and to Michael Joyce for giving me the confidence to take chances. Thanks to the 2014 Senior Composition class at Vassar and to my thesis advisor, Amitava Kumar, for the critical energy that propels stories forward. Thanks to some of my first "real" readers: Ethan, Rhea, Bridget. To Arman, for reading earlier drafts of earlier books that never made it out in print. And seeing something in them. To Sitara and Alice for the many ways they supported this book and made it better. To Isaac, Maria and Jinjoo for listening, always. And thanks to my mother, for always pushing for the difficult voices and the harder stories from home.

To some kick-ass primary and highschool teachers back in Joburg: Mrs Harvey, Mrs Gray, Mr McMahon and Ms Tommei.

The history of 1976 has been put together through oral narratives and texts from survivors, historians and educators. I am grateful to the authors of the books *Soweto Explodes*, by Maoala Mooogomi and *The Road to Democracy in South Africa: Vol II*, by the South African Democracy Education Trust, as well as to online sources such as South African History Online and *I Saw a Nightmare*, by Helena Pohlandt-McCormick, among countless other sources.

## PROLOGUE

# Jack

I DREAM OF ZANELE AT THE WHEEL, HER KNUCKLES AND FACE outlined by streetlights. We speed past vacant lots. She's driving too fast. Rain comes thick and heavy on the windows. It's the kind of storm that happens only on the highveld, the thunder loud and rapid. She doesn't speak. I need her to. Maybe she's counting the people who've died since we first met.

I calculate how fast the storm is coming up behind us—as if that helps. Zanele is taking us somewhere only she knows.

The things I am good at, lying and mathematics, are useless now. In the moments before the end, I can do nothing.

We crash onto the highway railing, the front chassis crumpling into the windscreen.

Another scandal, a black girl and a white boy found in a car with no explanation besides the obvious one.

THAT'S WHAT I DO NOW—SLEEP AND WAKE UP AND GO OVER things that have already happened or might have happened. I eat breakfast, a boiled egg and four slices of white bread, while I wait for a phone call that I know won't come. In Soweto, smoke rises from the shacks. Meena says that ever since the protest the police fire at plastic bags, animals, little boys—anything that moves. I read the newspaper over and over, thinking they'll mention Zanele. But they don't. The same footage on the protests repeats on the television. I call Meena at the shop and she tells me no news is good news.

I ask for less and less as the days pass. First, I wanted Zanele to apologize for all the things she didn't tell me, to apologize for disappearing without warning. Then all I wanted was for her to come back. Then it didn't matter if I didn't see her again. As long as she was alive.

# ONE

## Zanele

WE WERE GOING TO PUT DYNAMITE UNDER THE POWERLINE towers. There were three of us that day at the Orlando power station. Billy, Phelele and me. It was after school, and we'd come to make sketches—sketches that would show where the dynamite needed to go.

The power station's white caretaker explained how the electricity was generated and transported to the white areas of Joburg. As he talked he nodded and smiled, showing his dirty teeth. Billy nodded, flashing back his teeth, clean and white like an advertisement. Phelele and I looked at each other. The caretaker suspected nothing.

On the other side of the wire fence, children stared at us. They stood barefoot on long grass that had turned brown with the cold. Behind the fence and the children, the land dipped and rose. I could barely make out the road back to Soweto.

As we walked back, we saw rows and rows of corrugated roofs turned copper as the sun went down. And I imagined the Orlando power station exploding—the black bars of the towers flying apart and the lights going off in white people's homes. For a moment, it would be a blackened white city. It would warn the *mlungus* of what we would do if they didn't give us what we wanted.

IN HIS SHACK, BILLY MADE THE SKETCHES OF THE POWER station to send to the *Umkhonto We Sizwe* in Mozambique. They had explosives. They would slip back across the border and blow up the towers.

With a sharpened pencil, Phelele added arrows to the drawing to show where the dynamite should be placed.

They gave me the finished sketches. I had to drop them off at the train station. The envelope taped under the bench. I went alone, taking the path past the *shebeen* where Mankwe sang.

Before the power station, Billy, the meetings, I had just been Mankwe's sister, the Mankwe with the magic voice.

Now I was the sister who helped plant explosives.

AFTER BILLY AND PHELELE WERE ARRESTED, I WAITED FOR THE police to come for me. But they didn't. In court a month later, they and two others I didn't know were charged with terrorism. The court ruled that Billy had recruited students to join military cells in Mozambique that were plotting to overthrow the government.

Now the four of them, chained, are walked out of the court with their arms cuffed behind them. The cuffs are in the space between the sleeves of Billy's nice coat and his hands. I look away but I see the cuffs everywhere, metal glinting in the afternoon light.

Billy starts singing as he walks past us. *Asibe sabe thina.* I reach out and the blue fibre of his coat gets caught in my nails. Then the policeman pushes him. Billy's voice is low, soft, always the one the *gogos* in church liked best. We all join in with Billy, but Phelele is silent, head bowed. The policemen let us sing, because they don't understand what the song means. Or they don't care. They have Billy and Phelele. It doesn't matter if we sing that we do not fear them.

As the van doors slam shut, Phelele's eyes meet mine through the metal grating. This could be the last time I will see her. The policemen get inside the cab, red-faced and satisfied. The front doors close and the van pulls out. Everyone runs after it.

And I wonder who told the police about Billy and Phelele. "Come, Zanele." Vusi takes my shoulders, turning me away from the crowd. "Time to go home."

We walk past a long, clean black car. A blond yellow-haired man sits in the back seat, watching us and smoking. In the front, a black driver and a white policeman. I can't see their faces. Behind them, buildings form an outline of grey rectangles against the sky. Hillbrow Tower stands above the rest of the city. I've heard there's an elevator that takes you to a restaurant at the top.

We were thinking of targeting that too.

LATER THAT NIGHT, I PUT ON LIPSTICK AND GLITTER, AND SLIP into my sister's sequined dress. It is my night to sing at the shebeen. And I am back to being the person I used to be, before all of this happened.

## Jack

OLIVER, RICKY AND I GRADUATED FROM JEPPE HIGH SCHOOL last December and started crashing parties soon after. We didn't have anything better to do. Oliver was at Tucks for engineering, Ricky was "taking some time off" and "thinking of studying in the States" and I was free till August, when I'd leave for Oxford.

So far, we'd been to dozens of them, including a cabinet minister's birthday party and Miss South Africa's charity gala.

I was always the one who talked our way in. People wanted to believe me. Oliver liked the planning, planned more than we needed. And Ricky came along because he liked to boast in a casual way about what we'd done, how we'd got away.

At the gala last weekend, we tried on tuxedos and bad

American accents. We finished trays of champagne and skewered chicken because everyone there had been pretty boring. Miss South Africa even fawned over us for a few seconds, though Oliver was too nervous to say anything to her. Ricky thought she was average-looking. Later I went over to Megan's and told her that the whole thing had mostly been a waste of time.

I WAS HAVING DINNER IN THE GARDEN WITH MY PARENTS WHEN the phone rang. I left the table.

"I wish you wouldn't let Megan call at this time," my mother called after me. She didn't like Megan, but everything she said to me these days was easy to ignore.

I walked past the new television set. The phone was next to my letter from Oxford and a picture of my parents in the veld, my father holding her shoulder with one hand and a gun in the other. He had shot two kudu that trip and their heads were up there now, on opposite sides of the living room.

I picked up the phone.

"Ready for tonight, *bru*?" It wasn't Megan but Oliver. He sounded keyed up, bothered by something. Probably about his father finding out about what we'd been up to.

"What's tonight?"

"You're not going to believe—"

"What is it?"

"We're coming over."

I put the phone down and glanced at the television.

My father had just bought it yesterday. "Nineteen seventy-six, and the South African government finally allows its upstanding citizens to own a television," he'd said as the salesman put it in the boot of the car. "Jack, anything can happen now."

Out on the patio, my father ground a cigarette into his silver-green ashtray. He lit another while my mother fiddled with her wedding ring on her fine-boned fingers. The new maid came around and laid out dessert. My mother corrected her, using a patient voice. It had just turned six o'clock.

AT NINE, OLIVER ARRIVED WITH RICKY AND FOUR BOTTLES OF black face paint left over from last year's rugby matches.

They sat in my bedroom, Ricky fiddling with the case of new cufflinks my father had bought me.

"So?" I waited.

Oliver held up the face paint as if it explained everything. In his other hand he had a folded map.

"We're going to a shebeen." Ricky got up from my desk and flicked the glass cabinets that held my sports trophies. "In Soweto."

It had to be Oliver's idea. From the look on Ricky's face, I could tell he was daring me to back out. And backing out would be the safe, sensible thing to do. You didn't just go to Soweto—three white guys in an old Mustang, in the middle of the night. You just didn't.

"I'd rather not do the face paint," I said. "It's ridiculous."

"Come on Jacky boy, where's the fun?" Ricky said. "It's about dressing the part. I thought you'd love it."

"Not really," I said, but I took the bottle of face paint from Oliver's hand.

AS WE PASSED PARKTOWN, I TOOK THE TURNING INTO THE highway that cut through the city and down to the Cape. The Mustang's engine strained as we picked up speed. There was something off about the nights in Johannesburg. Too quiet. As if, emptied of all the blacks at night, the city shut down.

Next to me, Oliver opened out a map of the city in grid format with little red dots.

"Police raids," he said, tracing a path from one dot to the other.

I knew he wanted me to ask how he'd managed to steal the map from the police station.

"You think you'll be coming back after Oxford?" Oliver asked.

"Don't know," I replied.

"What I know is that this car's a piece of junk," Ricky said from the back. "Oxford boy or not."

"It's a Mustang, just leave it," Oliver said.

"My Ford runs way better," Ricky said. "And it's older."

"And where's your car, Ricky?" I asked.

"In the States."

Ricky came to Joburg four years earlier, because his father had got a high-up job at Anglo American. He still hadn't got over leaving the States, never would.

"So what drinks do they have there?" Ricky said. "I don't want any of that crappy beer. Can I ask for a gin and tonic, or will that be too fancy for them?"

"Ricky, I already told you," Oliver said. "All their stuff's really cheap."

"And once we're there, don't complain," I added. "No need to get a mob after us."

"They'll *moer* us," Oliver said. "Actually, the police will moer us too, if they find us."

"Your father will get us out if there's trouble with the police. No worries," Ricky said.

Obviously Ricky still didn't understand that Oliver would get in even more trouble because his father worked right under the police commissioner.

Oliver had probably organized all this to get back at his father without his father knowing it. That was the only way Oliver knew.

"We're not going to get caught, anyway," Ricky continued. "That's the point, right?" Ricky passed his flask of brandy over to Oliver. I braked for a traffic light. He lurched. Brandy spattered all over the back seat.

"No one talks to anyone except me," I said. I glanced at the map again, scanning our route. It got complicated once you got in the township. No road signs or street names marked on the map. I smelled the brandy, turned the air conditioner up.

"Where's the fun in that for us?" Ricky said.

"Guys, just be quiet," I said. "Nod. Can you manage that?"

"You think you're God, don't you, Jacky boy?" Ricky said.

"Show him, Jack. He doesn't believe you," Oliver said.

I took the turning into the Moroka Bypass. The lights were fewer and farther between now. Behind us, the rest of Johannesburg, its sheet of reds and blues, sank from view. Now, long yellow mounds of dirt on the side of the road—mine dumps—shone when the headlights glanced off them. I turned left at an old, deserted stadium.

"Okay," I said, catching Ricky in the mirror. "*Baas*, I just need ten rand for my grandmother. Just ten rand, baas Ricky."

"See, in the dark he'll sound just like a black. Just like one," Oliver said. "Our gardener Wilbur talks just like that."

"Okay." Ricky tapped Oliver's shoulder with a cassette. Oliver slipped it into the player. "You do the talking, as always."

The cassette started playing. This time it was Miles Davis, one of Ricky's new obsessions, smuggled in from the States in Ricky's suitcase. The music circled back and forth with its itchy blend of guitar and trumpet. The face paint felt sticky and wet on my skin.

I passed a wire fence in front of the Orlando police station. Two dim points of light behind the fence.

Oliver was quiet. We had entered Soweto now and there was no turning back. Not just yet.

• • •

I PARKED BETWEEN A CHEVROLET AND A FLASHY SILVER Chrysler without number plates. We walked around the walls of bent, corrugated metal.

The entrance was a six-foot-high hole. Two men stood on each side. Singing and shouting drifted out.

"Whose idea was this again?" I asked.

"Yours, Jacky, all yours," Oliver said. He was seconds away from running back to the car. I put a hand on his shoulder and pushed him forward. "No undercover police here to check you're out past your bedtime, promise."

Ricky pulled his hat over his face and pulled up his collar. I did the same, stepping in front of him. From my pocket, I took out three rand and slipped it to one of the bouncers, a fat man with a scar on his face and a good portion of his ear missing.

"They're with me," I said, keeping my voice low, the accent thick. The man looked at the money I put in his hand. For a moment he paused. Then he smiled and put the money in his pocket. Silent, Oliver and Ricky followed me inside, into a large, low-ceilinged room and the smell of beer.

"You tricked them, Jack." Oliver gripped my shoulder.

"Don't get too excited," I said, steering them to a corner. "We just paid him to let us in. Doesn't mean he's not going to tell his friends to take a shot at us."

On the left there was a bar counter, crowded with men spilling glasses of cheap beer. There was another smell too, that African beer they made from sorghum or something. A band played in front of us and couples danced across the narrow floor. The mikes were terrible, but the saxophone player and pianist were okay.

A young woman was singing with the band, and not well. Terrible pitch and no pace. In between songs, she made comments—a mixture of jokes and insults thrown at people she picked from the crowd. The audience seemed to enjoy this, though it was unclear why being insulted was so appealing.

"What's she doing?" Ricky put a hand over his face.

The singer's voice got louder. She was ignoring the music. The pianist tried to match her note for note, but she'd fall an octave or two and leave the guy scrambling. The sax guy just shook his head, laughed, and continued playing.

There was a man by the front of the stage who wasn't dancing. He wore a hat that kept his eyes in shadow, and a black suit with silver suspenders. In between songs, he scanned the room and exchanged nods with the bouncers. At the end of each song, he clapped loudly.

"Terrible music. Get me a drink, Jacky boy," Ricky said, waving his flask upside down. He hadn't painted the spaces around his eyes well. Even in the badly lit room, I could see white showing through. "I'm all out, and it doesn't look like I'll be able to handle this party sober."

That's when we heard the police sirens.

The people sitting at the bar sobered up very quickly. They jumped off their stools and made for the exit. On the floor, some men dragged their partners out. The others let go of the women and ran.

"Raid!" Everyone kept shouting, "Raid!"

Only the man with the wide-brimmed hat seemed untroubled. He took a position by the bar, crossed his legs and started another cigarette. "Make room for Zanele, Sunny," he said, his voice cutting over the chaos. The bouncer with the scar pushed people aside. The singer unplugged her microphone, put it down, and walked slowly out behind the others.

Because we were behind her, we got a path through the crowd too. The sirens were very close now, as were the sounds of pounding footsteps and car doors opening and closing.

The singer walked around the shebeen and into a side street, turned right and took a few steps down. We followed. Some others were already there, waiting it out. It looked like they were used to this kind of thing.

Oliver, Ricky and I took a place near the wall a yard or so away from the singer.

"Who were they looking for this time, Zanele? What did Thabo do this time?" one of the men asked, holding his knees. His breaths steamed up his large square glasses. Through the worn patches in his green sweater, thin elbows poked out.

"How would I know?" The singer took a place against the wall and crossed her arms.

Another man wearing an orange bow tie passed her his jacket. "Here *sisi*, take this." He said it like he was used to offering jackets to girls outside shebeens.

"You know Thabo very well, Zanele," said the man with the glasses. "Which means you know why the police are here."

The singer put on the jacket and ignored him.

We waited. Oliver slipped down against the wall and covered his face with his coat—terrified that his dad would find him here, even though he knew his dad was too high up in the police to go on raids himself.

I counted at least twenty men and five women standing around, including the singer.

Then we heard the sound of breaking glass.

"Aye, Sam. Sounds like Thabo is cleaning out his *umqombothi* for the police." The man with the glasses laughed.

"The police might as well drink it. Good whisky, some good beer. Do they think we are hiding guns between the bottles? What *domkops*," said the man with the bow tie.

"But what will the Black Berets do to Thabo for losing all their liquor?" asked the man with the glasses.

"I don't know, Professor, cut off something? An arm, if he's lucky," answered the man with the bow tie. "That's their style."

"Don't call me Professor."

"Too late, *bhuti*. All of Soweto calls you that."

The singer took off her shoes and dropped them to the

ground. There was something nervous, impatient about her.

"Zanele," said the man with the glasses, "What time is school tomorrow? Going to have to change out of those woman clothes now, aren't you?"

The singer said nothing, but turned her face toward the road, toward us, angry. She had high cheekbones and large eyes. Her eyebrows were thin and slanted. She was maybe seventeen or eighteen, but the make-up tried to hide it.

"Don't bother her, Professor," the one called Sam said. "Thabo will send his boys to give you a few *klaps*, and you won't like that."

"Thabo is being raided, so he might not last till tomorrow."

"Professor," the singer said, "try to teach your worthless lessons without falling down from all the whisky you've drunk. Your students never listened to you in English. Afrikaans is going to make you look like a fool. *Thula* and worry about your headache tomorrow."

The men in the alley laughed. The man with the glasses made for the singer.

"Be quiet, girl. Remember who your father was. No one like him with his whisky."

"Careful," the singer said. "You don't want to fight me."

The other men in the alley gathered behind her.

The man with the glasses tensed.

"Agh Zanele, you know Professor. He likes to tell us what to do. Just leave it."

Professor turned away from the singer and leaned back against the wall. Some laughed.

The sounds of the sirens were fading; the police were gone. Ricky nudged Oliver with his foot. We started walking away.

"*Ja*, now that was close. Pa would've slaughtered me." Oliver picked himself off the ground and followed me.

"Don't tell me we have to go back in there and listen to that terrible singing," Ricky said.

I laughed—forgetting for the moment that we were in a narrow space, that our voices were too loud, and that we were talking like the white people we were.

"What did you say?" The singer was behind me. She pulled my shoulder back. I smelled cheap perfume and hairspray. We were face-to-face now, and she took her time looking at me. There was glitter at the end of her fake eyelashes. Her make-up followed the sharp lines of her face, the high cheekbones, the thin, slanted brows.

"He doesn't like your singing," I said, in my black accent. "That's all."

The singer grabbed my collar. "Sam, Professor, look. Mlungu has painted himself black."

I jerked my collar out of her hand. It tore. And then Oliver, Ricky and I ran. We went through the alley, then turned left, breaking washing lines heavy with wet school uniforms. For all their drinking, the men behind us were fast. Ricky was falling behind.

And then, from somewhere, kids with stones in their hands. They ran after us, yelling "mlungu" and other things that I didn't understand.

"The car," I shouted to Oliver, who was ahead.

Oliver turned left. I threw him the keys as we ran out onto the road. The men and children chasing us were just a yard from Ricky now.

But Oliver had reached the Mustang. I heard him start the car, and then the headlights came into view, doors swinging open at the back. He turned and made as if to drive right into them. They fell aside. A stone hit the car's headlight, splintering flecks of glass. Oliver kept driving. I caught the roof frame and pulled myself onto the back seat. Ricky, panting, threw himself behind me. I closed the door.

The engine rattled as Oliver accelerated. He made for the highway.

"What a crappy car," Ricky said, between breaths. I ignored him, my shirt still smelling of perfume. There had been murder in that singer's eyes.

TWO

## Zanele

"Can you believe it? Three mlungu in black face paint. Even Professor helped us chase them out of Soweto. If I find him again, Mankwe, I will ring his neck like a chicken."

"Him?"

"Their leader."

"And what will that do?"

"Make him sorry."

My sister leaned back against the bedstead and smiled. She was pale and tired, her skin damp and cold.

"Ah, Professor doesn't like to run. So it must have been something serious."

I rolled up the plastic over the window. In front of us was all of Jabavu, its corrugated roofs and washing lines, red and pink clothes stretched out into the dawn.

"What are you thinking about, Zani?" Mankwe asked, turning on her pillow to look at me. Most of the time when she made jokes about Professor, I laughed. Now I was thinking about something else.

"I don't think the police took anybody."

"This time," my sister said. We both knew that, one of these days, Thabo was going to get caught. And there were so many kids tonight, it was difficult to know if any of them had been taken.

I stepped out of my sister's dress and laid it over the bedstead. It was four in the morning. School was in a few hours.

"How was the show?" Mankwe asked.

"What do you think? The same as it always is. Thabo just

stands there, I sing badly, and everyone either pretends that they don't know I sing badly, or laughs at me. Professor is ruder than usual because he's disappointed you didn't come."

"You are always picking a fight. It can't be that bad, Zani."

"It is." I put my hands on her forehead, then over her hands. She was in Mama's bed, and I hoped it would keep her warmer than our mattresses on the floor in the next room.

"Thabo didn't let you play the piano?"

"When does he ever let me play? He always has Solly. He might let me stand in for you, but not Solly."

It was funny how alike we looked, my sister and I, and how different we were. Creamy and rich, her voice poured into the shebeen and made you forget things you shouldn't. Made the shebeen boys think they were rich—even as they were spending the last of their wages on umqombothi. Even Professor spent all his money in the shebeen, so he could listen to Mankwe and pretend he wasn't a coward who followed the government's new baas law without question.

Before all this, he had been a student at Fort Hare. He'd gone around telling everybody that he was going to be a professor. The name stuck.

He would come in the evenings, stare at Mankwe's lashes in the dim light. Her voice would make him forget who he was. He loved to listen to Mankwe sing *Summertime*, an American song about having a rich father and a good-looking mother and fields of cotton. I don't know why Mankwe sang it so much. Mankwe didn't even know what cotton fields looked like.

Or it was *Sophiatown*. Mankwe could make you cry about a dead place over and over, and Professor's eyes would fill up.

Still, I shouldn't have said that to Professor, even though he had insulted Baba. Professor was scared of everything, even me, and everyone in that alley had known that.

"Go to bed," my sister said. "School tomorrow."

"When is Mama back?"

"Same as usual. Friday."

"Those new people are slave drivers."

"Agh, thula, Zanele. Go to sleep."

I took my hands away from my sister's forehead, hoping I'd sucked the cold from her for a little while. There were so many secrets Mankwe and I kept now, even from each other. Court cases and dynamite. I didn't know what her secrets were.

It started to rain. Now that it was pounding on the roof it was hard to sleep. All night, my mind kept turning over plans, and failed plans. Billy. Phelele in that police van.

That was a month ago and it felt as if the court case hadn't happened. I imagined Billy in a cell, repeating hymns to himself to keep sane. For Billy it would be hymns. There was something about the red brick of Regina Mundi Church, the long lines you had to wait in before entering, that he liked more than anything else. I hadn't been to that church since I was a child. Mama had stopped making the walk there on Sundays after Baba had left.

In the next room, my sister was still, except for the breaths going in and out of her body. Even though there was a leak in my mother's room, she didn't notice. That's the way she was. It took a lot to wake her up.

Thinking of Mankwe made me think of Baba. Like my sister, Baba could sing—Xhosa songs he remembered from his childhood, Zulu songs, English songs, and Afrikaans songs. On good days, he sang and drank, and everyone crowded into our shack. Everybody loved Jonas.

In my family, no one spoke Afrikaans like my Baba. He was young when he'd left home to work in the mines.

He made sure to learn the way the baas wanted things done. He learned quickly. It took him a long time to realize that the baas didn't care, would never care, no matter how hard he worked. By then, it was too late. His lungs were full of dust from the mines, his Afrikaans was perfect, and he was bitter.

I didn't know where he was now. Maybe still somewhere in the city, drinking and working out his last years. A tall dark man with ruined lungs. A walk that swung from side to side that I would recognize anywhere.

My mother's Afrikaans was good, but not like my Baba's. When you worked in someone's house like Mama did, doing their laundry and feeding them, sometimes you pretended that it was your laundry, your family. The few Afrikaans words you used were gentle. Mama must have liked the little children of the white family she worked for before this one. Marlene and Rosie. When they were little, they would see my mother coming and stream out of their house, white arms extended. "Nanny," they'd shout. "Nanny's home."

I used to have this plan about finishing university and living in the Bantustans, working as a lawyer. The only people I'd see were black. Black people would pay me my wages, I would buy my food from a black person—I wouldn't have to see a *Boer* for the rest of my life. Mama and Mankwe had let me plan. But, like everything else, what they told us about the homelands was very different from how it was.

Whatever I had, and whatever I would ever have was right here in this shack.

And of course the Boers always kept trying to make us more like them, but stupider, so that wherever we were, they'd own us. It was law now that all grade eight, nine and ten students had to learn everything in Afrikaans—and everyone, Thabo, Mankwe, Mama—expected me to ignore it. School had to be taught in Afrikaans so that we could serve tea better to the Afrikaner, say "*baie dankie*" every time he threw us a crumb.

I was in grade twelve, so the baas law didn't apply to me. I could finish my exams in English then graduate. Let the young ones take care of themselves. Agh, they'd survive.

I had been told all my life to agree with the Boer and his

police. So what if people disappeared and were never heard of again. Mama told us those stories all the time, to warn us. But Mama thought that her life, cleaning after white people who spent most of the time pretending she didn't exist, was a life worth living.

It was for Mama and Mankwe's own good that they knew nothing about what I was doing, what I had already done.

## Meena

TO MAKE SURE NO ONE MISTOOK HIM FOR A TERRORIST OR A communist, Papa had a picture of President Vorster in his shop. Vorster had a dreamy look on his face. His eyebrows were thick, his chin lumpy. At the other end of the shop, above the women's personal care shelf, there was a bad print of a Ganesh painting framed by a garland of fake marigolds. My grandmother had insisted on it.

Papa had not always been so eager to show his support for the government. When he was twenty, he'd been arrested for sitting on a whites-only bench with some of his friends as part of a political protest. They had waited hours for the police to come.

Papa spent two days in jail before his father paid his bail. Then he returned home with his father and went on making shoes as they always had. No more protesting. At least that's the way my grandmother told it to me. Papa never told me the story himself. My grandmother always ended the story with the admonition she'd given to Papa at that time. "Remember to be grateful for what you have, Meena. You might have been black."

From the outside, things hadn't changed much since then. Five minutes in that direction was Soweto, and blacks still came through here to get to the white parts of town. But there was something angry about our black customers now. The way they came in, ignoring the blacks-only entrance and slapping their change on the counter, made Papa nervous. He never said so, but I knew.

IT WAS A FEW MONTHS AGO, NEAR CHRISTMAS. WE WERE closing up shop and I had gone round the back to check on the rubbish. The water was running down the street, dirty and cold, getting into my shoes. And there was a boy there in a blue coat standing by the gutter and the row of dustbins, smoking.

Then he was gone. I walked over, wondering why he had been standing there like that when it was so wet. I looked down. On the ground, where the boy had dropped his cigarette, there was a pamphlet. I picked it up. On its cover was a black fist. The SASO. When I lifted the lid of our dustbin to throw it away, I saw more pamphlets, from the ANC and PAC—organizations that were banned.

I could have handed them over to the police. But I lifted them out and hid them in the shop.

PAPA HAD OPENED THE STORE IN 1971. TO HAVE A SHOP IN THIS area, he'd had to find a white man to sign that he owned it, a shadowy "Mr Hendriks" who was referred to my father by a friend. This Mr Hendriks would not meet Papa in person, but he'd sign the papers. Apparently he had no problem with Indians, as long as you paid him.

When the signatures had been approved, Papa was overjoyed, the happiest he'd been since Mama died.

The store was five years old now and still smelled of paint even though we've been lighting incense every morning since.

Five years, and the first time a policeman came into the store was yesterday, a few weeks after we'd doubled our order of instant coffee and coal. A black Mercedes drove up and the policeman came out while the black driver stayed in the car with a blond man in the back. The policeman stopped at the shop door and the bell rang. He stared at the radio, which was playing a concerto. Then at the garlanded picture of the elephant-headed god.

It was winter, but I could see the sweat on his neck and how his shirt stuck to his body. Slowly, I slid the pamphlets I was reading into my maths book and closed it. The policeman was watching me. I put my fingers over the maths book, and waited.

Papa was upstairs but I didn't call to him.

The policeman walked up to the counter and put his hands on its plastic surface, first one then the other. Then he sniffed.

"What is this smell, hey?" he said.

"Sorry, *Meneer*?"

"This smell, this disgusting smell."

I looked back at the policeman with the blankest expression I had. He leaned down so we were eye-level—I smelled sweat, saw pieces of tobacco in his teeth.

"Get me a packet of Lucky Strikes," he said.

I turned around, leaving the maths book on the table. Its cover propped open, slightly. Lucky Strikes, he'd said, even though he was a tobacco chewer. Lucky Strikes, I repeated to myself, just so I didn't panic. It was strange they'd sent the policeman to fetch the cigarettes, and not the black driver. Why had they done that? My hands slipped over the packs, and they tipped off the shelf. They made a soft crackling sound as they dropped to the floor, one after the other.

"What the hell did you do?" the policeman said. "I asked you a very simple thing."

I stood up with a pack in my hand. He snatched it from me and threw coins that fell onto the floor. Then he left.

"Incense sticks," I said to the empty shop.

The policeman leaned into the car and passed the cigarettes

to the blond man. Then he got into the back seat, and the car slid away from the curb.

Why was there an unmarked police car going through here? I didn't know then that I'd see the blond man again. But I should have guessed. I had a collection of illegal pamphlets. I was asking for it. The picture of Vorster could only do so much.

## Zanele

IN THE MORNING, THE SHACKS WERE WET FROM THE RAIN. Leftover drops slid from the roof and onto my face. I took my Baba's old jacket with the number 729 stamped in white on its back. It was the warmest we had. I went outside.

At the shebeen, broken bottles had been swept to the side of the street. The police would leave it alone for another few months, then return. I took the path past the shebeen. As I expected, Thabo's hand was on my shoulder before I came to the turn. Two boys trailed behind him.

I remembered a time when Thabo was one of the boys for a big *tsotsi* called Sizwe.

"*Suka*," he told his boys.

They ran off a few yards, then stopped, waiting for Thabo. "Two years and now I'm the boss, Zee," he liked to say.

"Morning, beautiful." He was wearing a new blazer with a shiny shirt under it.

"Save it," I said.

"You don't get that many compliments that you can turn them down, Zee." He took a packet of chewing gum from his pocket, a brand I didn't know, and offered me some.

"No?" He put a piece in his mouth, letting the silver wrapper fall to the ground. "Going to school?" he asked.

"Ja, so?"

"Zee, I didn't call the police to come to the shebeen. You sang and I didn't make jokes. And I did not invite the mlungu or the children for your solo performance. So don't be angry at me."

"You sure about that?" I said.

We walked up the hill and this time Thabo took the turning with me onto Mputhi Road. Three years ago, we'd part here to go to our different schools. Back then, Thabo dirtied his school shirts and shouted every stupid thing that came into his head. But after joining the Black Berets he started to dress like a *clever*. He still talked a lot, but there were some things he wouldn't tell me. Like whether he'd killed anyone yet.

After Thabo had joined the Berets, Mankwe and I told each other he was just playing around. It was not hard to believe. Thabo had a kind face. He still sometimes laughed like a child.

I had known Thabo for most of my life. He always said that I liked to act as if I were better than him, than everyone in Soweto.

"So, what about school?" he said.

"Why do you always ask me that?"

Thabo spat his chewing gum into the rubbish bin outside Winnie's house and opened a pack of Camels. "I've been hearing rumours about you people at Isaacson." He took out a cigarette and fished in his other pocket for a lighter.

"What does that mean?"

"Your friends are trouble."

"Friends?"

"Vusi, Billy. Masi," he said, as if those names were enough. "You like going around with them because they like you, say nice things. I understand—"

"No, you don't, *wena*."

Thabo waved his hands, ignored me. "They give you cigarettes when they're sitting in the bushes during school.

They say they will protest against Baas Education, stop this mess the government is making. You think they are just talking. But you have no idea what trouble they're going to get you in. Just because Mankwe doesn't notice doesn't mean I don't have eyes."

"I have eyes too. For all the wallets you steal from people on the train."

"Billy talked rubbish, and now he's in jail."

"Thula about Billy."

"Don't be one of those fools." Thabo leaned forward. "Keep your head down."

"You're not my baba, tsotsi."

"No. Yours ran away, fast as he could."

I pushed past him to the school gate and walked through. Then I heard his footsteps behind me.

"Sorry, Zee," he said.

"You think you're going to upset me by reminding me Baba left? That's old, old news."

"I'm looking out for you. And Mankwe and Mama Lillian. Just don't get into the kind of trouble you don't understand."

As if he understood anything about what we had been doing, Billy, Phelele and I. "Suka wena," I said. I kept walking.

Mr Mamphile, the history teacher, was leaning against the wall, watching Thabo, like most people watched tsotsis. "The school inspector is coming in today and you're late."

THE STARLITE CINEMA ON PRESIDENT STREET WAS EASY TO slip into. Vusi often told me to meet him there. I ducked past the ticket window. This time I wasn't caught by the usher. I walked into the middle of the three o'clock movie and sank into a seat. In front of me was a row of men and women, the light of the movie on their faces. On the screen, a black man played the piano and a blonde woman cried. *Casablanca*, again.

A boy in a gabardine coat and sunglasses sat next to me, a cigarette tucked behind his ear.

I hadn't seen Vusi since that day in front of the courthouse. He hadn't shaved since. "You need a haircut. And you should get rid of the sunglasses," I whispered.

After a while, his eyes fixed on the screen, Vusi said, "Zanele, I told you to wait, do nothing."

"That's what I'm doing," I said.

"Then why did I hear your tsotsi's shebeen was raided last night? That all the *abantwana* were running around at two in the morning with stones?" he asked in his soft, precise voice.

"I don't know why the children came."

"But they came, didn't they?" he said. "They listen to you. They know you sing at the shebeen." He put something in his mouth. "Zanele, remember how careful Billy was. And now he is in jail. And Phelele? We don't even know where they'll take her. We'll be lucky if we get the chance to go to her funeral."

"I'm being careful."

"It seems you sometimes forget."

"I haven't forgotten Billy. I think of him everyday."

"Masi is our face for the crowds. The police are already watching him. But you—" Vusi leaned closer. "—you are in the shadows. Like me. You get things done."

We'd come to the part in the movie where all the people in the bar stand up and sing some anthem with trumpets. Everyone except Ilsa, who does nothing. The sound was bad. I couldn't even hear the trumpets. We watched in silence.

Vusi took off his sunglasses. "You don't like the sunglasses."

"No one wears sunglasses to the movies," I replied.

He laughed. The old woman in front of us turned around and rapped him with a rolled-up newspaper. "Thula, we are watching a movie. Go make trouble somewhere else."

Vusi slid farther down in his seat and rubbed his knee. "Anyway, I have a job for you."

"What?"

"You need to find the ones in each school who will help us to organize this protest against Afrikaans. We want all the abantwana out on that day. All of them."

"What about Billy? Phelele?"

Vusi turned away from the screen. "You tell me." Then he turned back to the screen, took another sweet from his pocket. I heard it cracking between his teeth. "They are gone now. We turn our attention—"

"Turn our attention?"

The old woman turned around again now to glare at me, newspaper still in her hand.

Vusi waited until she had turned back around. "Yes." He rose and dropped the bag of sweets on my lap. "Enjoy the movie. And remember, you are in the shadows."

JUST BEFORE ILSA LEFT BOGART, I WALKED OUT OF THE CINEMA and crossed the street into a store called Pillay's All Purpose. Vusi said it was safer to leave a meeting place at different times and stop at different places along the way back.

I pushed open the door and the bell made a tired sound. I had never been in there before. My sister said that the owner was grumpy and always cheated. From the radio, a concerto played. The violin, muffled but determined, rose with the piano to a crescendo. There were crates of spices, dried fruit packets, *mealie* meal. Incense sticks.

"Can I help you?" There was a thin Indian girl at the counter with long black hair in a plait. She watched me walk past the shelves. Above her head, Vorster in a frame.

"I'm just looking. Don't worry. I have money to pay," I said, looking up at Vorster.

"I never said that," she said.

I walked down the makeup aisle.

"I wouldn't advise buying that face cream. It's not good."

I put the cream onto the counter. "You sell things you know aren't good?"

"Where do you go to school?" she asked me.

"You didn't answer my question."

"Sometimes." She closed the cash register. "So, which part of Soweto are you from?"

"I'm not here to answer your questions." I turned to leave.

"You're not going to school because of the baas laws?"

"What do you know about that?"

"I read some things."

"What things?"

"And I've seen you walking up and down this road for a few weeks now."

"You've been watching me?"

The girl tried to avoid my eyes and said nothing. On the radio, the last strains of the violin dimmed, and the announcer's voice came on and told us we'd just listened to Dittersdorf's *Concerto in C major*. On the shelf behind the counter, there were piles of newspapers, yellowed and years old. *The Rand Daily Mail* and *The Star*. A few copies of *The World*, *The Sowetan*, *Drum*.

"No—" Her eyes widened, looking at something behind me. I heard a door open and close upstairs—I turned and looked outside, saw nothing but the same pavement, the same traffic, some black car against the pavement, a cigarette butt dropped on the ground.

"Take it. It's more yours than mine anyway."

Something hard and square under my hands, like a box. Footsteps on the stairs.

A man appeared at the stairs. He stopped when he saw me opposite the register.

"Meena, why did you leave the counter?" he called.

The Indian girl had slipped past him, her braid swinging behind her. Her eyes darted from the window. Then fixed on my hands. A book. Grade 12 Pre-calculus. Her lips tightened.

"It's not—"

"I'm sorry we can't help you," she said in a different voice, but her eyes were scared.

Her father took a step closer to me, like he was going to drive me out the shop.

I shrugged and left.

Outside, I opened the book. Definitely not my book, or a book anyone in Soweto had. Too new. Folded inside it an ANC flyer about a meeting. Slipped in between the pages more ANC notices. One was for a SASO meeting next week.

Through the shop window, I saw the Indian man at the counter watching me.

How had that Indian girl got hold of the pamphlets?

THREE

# Thabo

My favourite nights were the ones when Mankwe was sick and Zanele had to do the show instead. It was not that I wanted Mankwe sick. No.

When Zanele came instead of Mankwe, the regulars weren't happy, but who cared about them? I chose who played at the shebeen, because Sizwe had made me manager.

And sometimes Zanele came to play the piano when Solly was not in town. Then it was both of them, Mankwe at the microphone and Zanele at the piano. Solly had taught her some chords last year near Christmas. Zanele loved the blues and her piano playing was much better than her singing. But when Zanele was playing, all she could see was her sister. She never looked at me.

Of course, in my business, it was stupid to put the one thing that mattered to you on stage in a red dress for everyone to see. Even back then I knew that.

I'd been running after Zanele for years, and because she ignored rather than laughed at me, like she did when some of those other *bafana* chased her, we just carried on doing the same thing. Which was nothing. Like she said. Old news.

What was new was Zanele hanging around President Street after school. Where Billy, Vusi and the rest smoked other people's cigarettes and talked about fighting the government, revolution, all that *kak*. But Billy was in jail now. Not my problem.

I didn't exactly tell the policemen about Billy. What kind of fool gets caught talking to *abo gata*? There was a local informant, and he wasn't hard to find. There was only one man who wasn't a tsotsi who tried to dress as nicely as me around here, Sam Shenge. He spent the money the police gave him on blue and orange bow ties. Everyone knew the money for his bow ties didn't come from the wages he earned taking pictures for any newspaper that would take them. Any fool could see that, but they chose not to.

The wisest thing Sizwe had ever told me was: be nice to your friends, nice to your mama, and nicest of all to the abo gata. But Sizwe didn't know that I earned a little something on the side from telling Sam about the boys and their stupid plans. When I heard the rumour about Billy planning to blow up the power station, I got five rand for passing along rubbish about something that was less likely to happen than the sun falling on our heads. The abo gata actually believed the crazy stories about Billy, because next thing I know Billy's arrested and there's a big court trial for him and that pretty girlfriend of his.

That was not a problem for me. Actually it was a good thing. Now Sam and the abo gata thought I knew who the real troublemakers were.

But now that Zanele was making friends with Billy's friends, my business with Sam was going to be trickier. Here she was hanging around President Street, even though I had warned her to stay away from here. I thought about dragging her back home. I wanted to. But Zanele didn't work that way.

Some trouble got you a fine, some sent you to Robben Island with that old man Mandela, and some got you killed. Maybe I was thinking too much about the kinds of things Zanele might be doing.

So I waited for her to walk out of sight, then I walked to Pillay's to get the owner to pay us. He earned good money. But like most of the Indian shopkeepers around here, he treated us like we were dirt under his shoes. It was going to be an easy job to convince him. I could have sent one of my boys.

Inside, Pillay was there behind the counter, and so was his daughter. I'd bought cigarettes here many times before.

There was no security, a little lock at the cash register. Useless. I walked in.

"Please, sir. No smoking." Pillay was big on his "sirs" and "pleases." He didn't recognize me. Disappointing, for a store owner on President Street not to be able to tell the difference between a clever and a boy still in school. The girl just stood there. She was wearing her school uniform, which was too big for her.

"I've been watching you, Mr Pillay," I said. "Watching for a long time."

"Please, sir. No smoking," Pillay repeated.

"You've been earning your money off us for years."

I ground the cigarette on the newspaper on the counter. The paper caught fire for a second or two, flaring up into yellow. Then it went out.

"Sir. I think you should leave," Mr Pillay said.

"No. So as I was saying, you make good money. And do I have a problem with this? No." I shrugged. "Me and my boys, we are simple people. If a man is earning some money, white, Indian, black, good for him."

Pillay turned to the girl, who'd stopped reading her newspaper. "Meena, go upstairs."

"No," she said, and watched me like she couldn't see enough of a black man in a nice suit.

"But then I realized," I continued, "the reason why your business is doing so well." I lit another cigarette. "My boys and I are keeping your store and your family safe."

Pillay looked at my cigarette and said nothing.

"Don't you think that we should have a share of your earnings, Mr Pillay? Isn't that something we deserve?"

The man just watched the cigarette smoke. The girl froze.

The man folded the newspaper where I'd put my old cigarette, and put it into the dustbin. "You know that some people like you came here six years ago. I said the same thing I'm going to say to you now. No. You're working for someone, aren't you? Who?"

"Sizwe. The Black Berets." I leaned forward. I could see the places on his face where his light brown skin had sunk in. The name "Sizwe" meant something to him.

I put a hand over my left jacket pocket. "I don't want to make things bad for you, Mr Pillay. Or your family." And I looked at his daughter.

"Get out!" Her voice went high, cracked at the end.

Then quietly Mr Pillay said, "How much?"

"Ten rand, and guess what? I'll only make you pay once a month, as a special favour."

A little girl came running down the stairs. She had long hair like her sister. She was maybe six, seven years old. She hid between her father's legs and made faces. I winked at her. She giggled.

Pillay handed the money to me slowly, like it was his blood. Indians can be like that with money. I looked from the little girl to the older one. Then I pocketed the money and left.

"We'll call the police." The older girl had followed me down the street. I turned around, and she looked scared. She didn't know not to run after a tsotsi. Her father started running and shouting after her. I stared at her, then at her thin father, and laughed.

# Meena

MY GREAT-GRANDFATHER STOOD BAREBACKED AND BLACK against the grey of the dock. He was in a line of Indian men walking toward the outline of sails. It was 1860. In a few minutes, they would board the SS *Belvedere*. Begin to know the rough grain of the wood on their skin as the ship rocked. Twenty people would die of cholera on that ship before it docked in Natal. But he would survive. A pen sketch of the ship is framed in our upstairs room, a sign for my grandmother of promises made and kept.

There were many Indians, like my great-grandfather, who were lured across the sea to work in fields of sugarcane. Now my dad bought large bags of sugar to sell in the store.

So yes, I was a descendant of desperate people who had come looking for a better life. I didn't usually think like this. Most of the time, I was thinking of bones and blood and incisions, school exams and being irritated doing shifts at the store. The way the cash register drawer always seemed to jam. Why didn't Papa for God's sake get a new one? But the tsotsi's visit had changed things. His burgundy vinyl shoes. The sound of them against the floor as he walked away from the counter with our money in his pocket. His laugh. He'd said he was from the Black Berets, but he wore a fedora.

At dinner, Papa didn't say anything about the tsotsi to my grandmother. But of course, Jyoti kept asking about him, calling him the fancy man. Like he was an old friend of ours who had dropped by to give her a treat. I told her to keep quiet, but that only encouraged her.

Papa helped himself to more food and ate as if he'd completely forgotten the tsotsi.

I got up from dinner, putting a last piece of roti in my mouth.

"Falling out, it's falling out." Jyoti pointed at the roti.

My grandmother made a disapproving noise.

"Where are you going?" Papa asked.

"Out. Study group."

Papa said nothing. The mid-year exams were coming, and Papa knew as well as I did how hard you had to work to get into medical school. The idea that his own daughter might become a doctor gave him something to look forward to.

Study group was the best thing to say when I was going to a SASO meeting, and Krishni and her brother Prinesh were good camouflage. Krishni was also trying to get into medical school. Prinesh, who was older, with his neatly groomed hair that shone from hair oil, liked telling people that he had met special requirements and was already at Wits University. My grandmother liked repeating the same nice things about Prinesh every dinner.

Prinesh told me when the SASO meetings were happening—even though he knew my grandmother and father disapproved. I don't even know why he went to the meetings. He never really talked about politics. He just agreed with whatever anyone else said.

It was a twenty-minute walk from President Street to Wits. We took Rissik Street, skirting past old, red-brick office buildings with their elaborate hooded entrances and newer buildings that smelled of paint and cement. Every few minutes or so, headlights from cars flared up behind us. Ever since the tsotsi came, I kept thinking that every car, every footstep was him or one of his men. Tossing their cigarettes, picking their nails with knives.

I needed a plan for when he came next.

The campus was quiet when we got there. We stopped at corners of cement-and-brick walls and watched for policemen.

Because of the arrests over the past few weeks, the SASO meeting days changed often. Last week there were four policemen standing outside the back entrance of Senate

House. They hadn't questioned us. To be neither black nor white was to have different, unclear loyalties. It wasn't assumed that we were political agitators.

And anyway, Prinesh always seemed so innocent.

Still, it was worrying that the police had sent four policemen to disrupt what was, for now, still a legal meeting.

We circled from the back of Senate House to its front, passing the long flat steps below the pillared façade.

PRINESH PICKED SEATS AT THE BACK AS A SMALL GROUP OF university students collected at a table that held a thermos of coffee. They poured the coffee into plastic cups, not noticing how some of it dripped to the floor and onto their shoes. I scanned for missing faces. Of the usual four people chairing the meeting, one was missing. A smaller man had taken his place. He stood at the table, his eyes darting to different points in the room. He hadn't taken off his beanie, which looked dusty. I imagined he was the kind of man who didn't sleep in beds, but in hidden spaces. A man who wasn't supposed to be here. Not officially.

Ten minutes later, younger students burst through the door and took seats at the front. On the left side of the front row two students in blue cardigans sat on either side of a guy in a loose, green-and-yellow printed shirt that went to his knees. He was having a good time, nodding at people he knew, his arms spread over the backs of the chairs next to him. The boys either side of him were silent, strangely alert, as if they were his bodyguards. One of the boys had a pair of sunglasses resting above his forehead. The girl who I'd given my pamphlets to wasn't here. It was silly to imagine she might be.

I learned later that the boy in the printed shirt was the one who everyone would follow on the day the protests started. His name was Masi Ngumede.

But all I knew then was what I had read in the newspaper

the previous week. A judge had sent four students from Morris Isaacson School to jail for planning to blow up the Orlando Power Station with help from trained ANC operatives in Mozambique—the Umkhonto We Sizwe. Some of the SASO members at this meeting must have been working with them. But something had gone wrong.

Like me, Prinesh was staring at the students sitting at the front. He looked scared.

"What's the problem?" I asked. He didn't reply. A light film of sweat had collected over his narrow cheeks and forehead, his small moustache. The sweat made his face look like a mask.

The man with the beanie at the front stood and saluted the students. Then he slapped the table. "The Afrikaans Medium Decree Act." He slapped it a few more times. "Forcing the language of the oppressors on our brothers and sisters here. Making sure that they will be servants to the Afrikaner. Do we accept this?"

"No." People stood up. "No, no, no!"

"We're leaving. Now," Prinesh said, pushing Krishni in front of him and trying to do the same with me. I shrugged him off, but followed. We pushed past the crowded room to the exit, Krishni accidentally tipping over the thermos. I picked it up. Eyes on me, including the boy with the green and yellow shirt, and his friend with the sunglasses. I wasn't sure they wanted me here. And we went out into the street. I felt the coffee bleed through my clothes. Krishni and Prinesh walked ahead, fast, but I lagged behind, nervous, angry.

And not just because Prinesh had forced us to leave the meeting early.

All I could do was sit in the shop, study, collect pamphlets, pictures of Steve Biko's determined face, with his large forehead. He's a doctor too, I wanted to tell my father. But I never would. Somewhere out there was the book of pamphlets that I'd thrust into a stranger's hands. All I could do was wait.

Maybe it was better that I had given the girl my pamphlets. After I'd seen the car again, I knew I should never have kept them. If she tried to report me, I could turn the story on her. As my grandmother liked to say, police would always believe an Indian over a black.

The two figures ahead of me were toy-sized pieces in the dark. I ran to catch up.

## FOUR

## Zanele

THAT NIGHT IT RAINED AGAIN. THIS TIME I FELT IT ON MY FACE and shoulders—a new leak in the roof. I brought over a pot to catch the drops. The rain made a tinny sound as it hit the metal bottom. That was when I saw Masi at our door.

It was strange to see him here, alone. He spent most of his time with Vusi, planning things.

"Why are you here?"

"Billy is back," he said. The ends of his eyes were pinched together. Because of the rain, but also because he was happy.

"You're joking."

"They just released him, Zanele." He took my hands and pulled me to the street.

The rain came down on our heads as we ran out on the mud roads, screaming. Mothers with baskets on their heads stared at us as we ran.

"Masi, enough splashing now," I said, slowing down. He didn't listen.

Masi had come to tell me first. He knew I cared about Billy like he did.

BILLY'S FAMILY HAD THE ONLY PURPLE SHACK IN THE STREET, but we couldn't see its colour in the dark. It was larger than the others too, even though only Billy and his grandmother lived there now. There was no light in the shack when we came to the door, and no one answered when we yelled and knocked. We went around to the back, and Masi pushed himself through the broken rusted door and fell onto the floor. I followed.

"Who's that?" a voice came from the other side of the room, and then a candle was lit.

There was Billy in his bed, a knife in his hand. He was much thinner, still in his blue wool coat. But the coat was old and torn now.

"Welcome back, bhuti." Masi held out his arms.

Billy's eyes darted from me to Masi. But he didn't put away the knife. "Leave," he said.

"What did they do to you? Where's Phelele?" I asked, stepping closer to the light.

Billy flinched.

"Billy, we just came to see you," Masi said, like he was talking to a small child. "Sorry we woke you. We were too happy."

"Both of you are stupid," Billy said in a low, hissing voice I'd never heard before. "Don't you know they are watching this house, watching all the people who come here?"

"Okay," I said in a voice only Billy could hear, "we will meet you somewhere else."

"Don't you understand?" Billy said. "I don't want to see any of you again. Stay away from me." He got to his feet and waved his knife. His gogo came into the room and just stared at us, saying nothing.

Masi backed up against the wall. "Zanele," he said, pressing his finger to his lips. He went back out through the door. For a few seconds I waited, hoping that Billy would tell me all this was a joke. But he didn't. The door scraped my arm as I followed Masi out.

We walked home, our bare feet splashing through pools of muddy water. "I was stupid to go there," he said.

"No, you weren't," I said, but I didn't sound as if I believed it.

AT HOME, MANKWE WAS STILL SLEEPING BEHIND THE CURTAIN. I lit the candle next to my bed and opened the Indian girl's maths book, trying to forget Billy. I ran my fingers over the detailed graphs, the index. The pages were thick and creamy.

In between them, enough manifestos from banned organizations to give me five years in jail. She had everything in there, notices from the ANC, PAC announcements, an assortment of trade union pamphlets, the latest SASO issue. Usually, people chose one organization to support.

Billy had once told me to be careful about traps like this. But Billy was gone. So was his advice.

Tucked inside the SASO issue there was a black-and-white picture of Steve Biko, its founder. The picture had no caption, and seemed to have been cut out of something else.

I didn't hear her come in. "Mama." I looked up at her. Her bag was wedged under her arm. The cloth she wore around her head was wet from the rain. There were deep lines around her eyes and mouth. But the skin on her forehead was smooth, like a child's. For a long time, she stared at the pamphlet on my lap and said nothing.

"You didn't go to school today," she said. "You are meeting those boys. One of them has already gone to jail. You want to get yourself killed?"

"Thabo told you. You know Billy has come back? Thabo just sees what he wants to see."

"Zanele. Stop this." She waited.

I said nothing.

Parting the curtain, she walked through to check on Mankwe. "Get ready to come with me to work tomorrow, Zanele," she said. "They're having a party."

MAMA HAD BEEN WORKING FOR A NEW FAMILY SINCE JANUARY. The old family, the Van Nierkerks, had moved to Cape Town. Mama had worked for them for fifteen years. She used to say it was a good job. Sometimes she brought Mankwe with her. Sometimes she brought me too.

"Isn't Mankwe a pretty girl? And with the voice of an angel," Mrs Van Nierkerk would say. "Lillian, why don't you take this old dress of mine and fix it up for her? You're so blessed to have such a pretty daughter. Look how she plays with the kids. All the boys will want to marry her."

A few nights before they left, the Van Nierkerks had a farewell party. Mankwe went with Mama, to help. They came back at two in the morning, carrying foil-covered plastic containers filled with cold chicken leftovers and sausages with herbs.

Mama had said nothing about the new family.

WE TOOK THE BUS IN THE AFTERNOON. MAMA ALREADY HAD my passbook signed and stamped. She must have taken it from under my pillow.

We didn't say anything during the bus ride. Nothing about school or my sister. Nothing. I looked out of the open window and breathed in the fumes from the highway. We were close to downtown now—to the yellow-grey-tinted office windows and bright, newly painted cement.

Slowly, the buildings gave way to lower roofs of sloping slate and wood surrounded by quiet gardens.

I hadn't been in a Putco bus for a while. I almost forgot the packed bodies next to me, the loud conversations. It felt good, even though the woman on my other side was resting her melon on my lap.

THE CRAVENS HAD A MUCH LARGER HOUSE THAN THE VAN Nierkerks. On one side was a thick-trunked tree. It had been clipped in places, but some of its leaves drooped low to touch the grass. Underneath was a small, rusted slide. This made me think there had been a child here once.

Mama and I entered by the front gate, where the security guard let us in. They didn't say anything to each other, which was strange.

Mama's room was behind the house. It smelled of orange-scented air freshener and had beige carpets and blank white walls.

"No decorations," I said.

"No decorations." Mama took off her coat.

I took off Baba's, and we put them on the bed. We walked through the back door and then the living room. The first thing I noticed were the eyes of the kudu on the wall. They were large and black and glittered, as if water was trapped inside them. The second thing I noticed was that the house smelled of varnish.

Mrs Craven was in the kitchen. She was running her fingers over the shelves, checking for dust. We stood, waiting for her to finish like we had nothing better to do than to stare at her narrow back. Her dark hair was shiny, and she was wearing what were nice clothes for white people.

Finally, she looked up. She saw me and stepped closer. She was so small that Mama and I stood head and shoulders above her.

I wanted to say, "Come, Mrs Craven. Come closer. Touch my face and check for dirt."

"What is your name?"

"Zanele."

"And how old are you?"

"Eighteen."

"You drink?"

"No."

"No drinking here, understand?"

"Yes."

"You have boyfriends?"

Mama nudged me.

"No."

"Boys are not allowed to come into the maid's quarters. Under any conditions. You understand me?"

I didn't answer for a long time, long enough for Mrs Craven to understand what I thought of her. "Yes. No boyfriends. No alcohol," I said. "And no stealing."

Mrs Craven turned to my mother. "Lillian, I am only hiring her this time. Make sure she behaves herself."

Mama looked from Mrs Craven to me. "Yes," she said finally, wishing she had Mankwe with her instead, who knew to take orders quietly and took half the time to clean.

"The chicken must be sautéed in olive oil before adding garlic. I want all the cocktail glasses properly cleaned. Mop all the floors, starting from the porch." Mrs Craven left the kitchen. "And remember the *koeksisters*," she called from the next room. "I'm trusting those to you, Lillian."

We took the mops out onto the patio and took turns sinking them into the bucket of water and wringing them out. I expected Mama to tell me not to speak to Mrs Craven like that, but she said nothing. There was only the sound of the cloth against the tiles and the spray of dirty water that hit me when Mama plunged her mop in the bucket too fast. It was better than I had expected, to work there alone with Mama— no sign of the family that lived in this house.

# Jack

MR AND MRS VAN ROONEN HAD HEAVY, ROUND FACES. OUT on the patio, they chewed olives and cheese off toothpicks, and said nothing. My father kept laughing, as if one of them had just cracked a joke. No one seemed to find this strange.

My father was trying to sell beer. Before that, he had

sold car parts, but he said he "needed to diversify." Mr Van Roonen worked in the Trade and Industry division for the Bantustans—exclusively black areas. A place, my father said, where alcohol flowed like water.

Now he wanted Mr Van Roonen to help him get a permit to sell beer there. And if it meant pressing food on Van Roonen and laughing while he ate it, well, that was easy.

Up until now, the Van Roonens hadn't said much. My father continued laughing at nothing, and my mother joined in. Usually it was the other way around. I took another Castle out of the cooler box, avoiding the cans of Trident, the beer my dad was trying to sell. He had a warehouse twenty minutes away, with stacks of it.

I'd probably inherit it when he died.

"Mariaan and Johan, come inside for some dinner." My mother waved them in. She was trying hard, and it showed.

We sat at the dining table. The recent varnish made its surface feel greasy. Mother had tried to keep it simple, chicken and beans and sausages. The maid came in carrying a serving dish, and her helper came around with a jug of water. After filling Mrs Van Roonen's glass, I saw her face.

She turned to my father, offered him a glass. She was wearing an apron and there was a white cap on her head, but it was her. The singer from the shebeen.

Everyone at the table suddenly became loud.

"Yes, yes, Mr Craven, I agree that the black man likes to drink his beer. We are not contesting that."

"There would be handsome revenue for the government."

"Handsome?"

"High profits for the government. It would create jobs," my father said, leaning forward and flashing his smile.

"White jobs or black jobs, Mr Craven?"

"Johan, we wouldn't be here if I wasn't promising jobs for whites."

The singer hadn't looked at me directly yet. Maybe she didn't recognize me.

But then she did.

The first thing that showed on her face was surprise. Then her expression flashed to the one she'd had when she'd set all her friends on us outside the shebeen. She continued around the table slowly. When she came to me, she leaned down, holding the jug. For a moment we were close, this time no perfume, and she whispered, "Don't worry, mlungu. I haven't forgotten who you are."

Her voice in my ear, at my dinner table, shocked me.

The maid walked in with another tray of food. The singer straightened and left with the jug.

Mr Van Roonen started sounding more enthusiastic around dessert. The koeksisters cheered Mrs Van Roonen up, so maybe my mother's attempt at serving something Afrikaans might have secured my father's deal. As for me, I tried not to look at the singer for the rest of the meal.

Koeksister or no, it wouldn't be great for my father's beer business if the Van Roonens learned that I liked to spend my spare time in shebeens. But she wouldn't dare.

Just as I was finishing off my first koeksister, the doorbell rang and Megan walked straight in.

The Van Roonens turned from their sausages to look at her. My mother tensed.

The singer walked in with an extra plate and cutlery. Megan sat down. I concentrated on my plate as the singer put a napkin next to Megan.

"Thank you," Megan said in a low, clear voice. The singer didn't make any sign that she'd heard.

As I kept chewing and swallowing, I was aware of the singer weaving around the table, her apron brushing its edges. In the background, my dad's voice rose, offering to sell Trident at a lower starting price, to increase sales and tax revenue.

Then the singer finally left. I didn't see her for the rest of the meal.

Megan pointed her fork at Van Roonen. "Do you really want to introduce even cheaper liquor to the Bantustans, when alcohol is breaking their families?"

My mother got angry.

My father smiled. "Megan, dear, you don't understand. It all boils down to the bottom line—creating revenue where demand already exists. Revenue means bread on the table for the family. The black one and the white one."

"I don't think that's how it works," Megan said. Her father was an editor at the *Rand Daily Mail*, so Megan thought she knew about these things.

My father didn't bring up Trident for the rest of the evening.


## Zanele

It was the same mlungu from the shebeen, because he almost choked when he saw me.

I sat on Mama's bed, waiting for them to finish eating, so we could clean up. The boy's mother told us to wait until she called us. That Afrikaans man ate a lot, and the boy's family laughed at everything he said. The boy said very little, and smiled like he agreed with everything that was said.

This meal was going to take some time.

The door opened and the mlungu stood there. Because he was tall, he took up most of the doorway, blocking the light from the corridor. He had a neat haircut and expressionless eyes. You could tell he was very pale but spent time at the beach to hide it.

He wasn't in a hurry to say anything.

I looked at his hands. He put them in the pockets of his trousers, stretching the fabric.

"You're not allowed to be here," I said.

"Sorry," he said. His voice was more careful now than that time at the shebeen.

"So why are you waiting here? Go finish your dessert. Those Boers are waiting."

"I will, don't worry." He smiled, stopped leaning against the doorway. "Look, we both know why I'm here."

"I don't know. Maybe you are here to show me the real colour of your face, in case I got confused at the shebeen."

"Look. That was just some face paint. It was just one of my friend's stupid jokes, nothing more."

"My mother and I will come here next time with our faces painted white," I said. Then, imitating his voice, "It will just be a stupid joke."

He said nothing for a while, his eyes fixed on my face. "Look, I'm sorry." Then, in a more hesitant voice, a voice that I didn't trust, he continued. "Anyway, it wouldn't be a good idea to mention what happened."

"Why? Because the government people would like to know you go to shebeens in your spare time and paint your face."

"Look, there's no reason to create a scene." His voice had become soft and even. It was hard to tell what he really meant.

I got up from the bed.

"I'm sure I could also make it worth your while," he said, reaching for his wallet.

I pushed the door hard and it hit him.

I SHOULD HAVE TAKEN THE MONEY FROM THE MLUNGU. THE problem was that I was too proud for Soweto, too proud for Johannesburg. The whole of Africa. That's what Thabo said.

# Jack

I FELL, TRIPPING OVER THE METAL STRIP OF THE DOOR FRAME, just as the maid entered the corridor. She stopped in front of the door to the maid's room, waiting for me to leave, her expression carefully neutral.

I got up and walked back to dessert.

It had been the wrong move to offer the singer money. The wrong move entirely.

I ONLY SAW HER ONCE MORE THAT WEEKEND. THE MAID'S CAP was tight around her forehead, covering her hair and the tops of her ears. She was at the piano in the second living room. She had a duster under her arm, and was pressing down the keys, but she stopped right before they made a sound.

No one usually came into this room. The sofas were high backed and uncomfortable. There was an old, dusty impala head on the wall. And there were souvenirs with the queen's face, everywhere—my mother's collection.

"Know how to play?" I asked.

Of course she didn't reply. She wiped the piano keys with a rag and lowered the lid. As she left the room, she passed me with that same silence she had at dinner.

FIVE

## Meena

THE BLACK MERCEDES CAME AGAIN TO STOP FOR CIGARETTES. As I waited for the car to park, I put down a larger order for Lucky Strikes for next week, since it looked like Pillay's All Purpose had acquired another loyal customer. I had told Papa that police had come for cigarettes, and all he said was good, it would keep the tsotsi away. I brought a pack down from the shelf, but this time it wasn't the policeman, but the driver, coming out of the car.

He walked in and rubbed his hands as he entered, leaving the door propped open. Through the shop window I watched the blond man in the back seat lean out of the car, tap the ash of his cigarette onto the sidewalk. He met my eyes.

The driver walked slowly to the counter, taking off his wool cap to reveal grey patches of hair. I held out a pack of Lucky Strikes. He smiled, and I wondered at what. His eyes were sunk in their sockets, but bright. He had a faint rash on his neck, with small distinct spots.

"Please, two," he said.

I went to get another. Unlike the policeman, he didn't seem in a hurry. I got a second pack and put them both on the counter. He got his wallet out of his pocket and started singing along to the radio, which was playing a James Brown song. His voice was deep and raspy, but musical.

"This is good music you have here," he said.

"Thanks," I said, and before I could think about whether it was a good idea or not, I asked, "Your boss, he likes Lucky Strikes?"

The man chuckled, then coughed. "Yes, he likes them, I like them too." The policeman who chewed tobacco was the odd one out.

He fingered through his wallet, then eased out two notes and put them on the counter. He took the packs, then dropped one, coughing. Picking it up, he took a hanky from his pocket and pressed it to his mouth.

"Aye, Jonas. Come now, enough of the chatting," the blond man called out from the car.

The driver turned to leave. "Ja, baas, I'm coming." As he left the shop he flashed a smile at me, leaving the door open.

I went to close it and watched the car join the traffic.

# Thabo

LAST NIGHT, PROFESSOR ASKED TO BORROW SOME MONEY. I hadn't seen him borrow money from anyone, not even Sam Shenge, who often sat next to him in the bar. Professor came to the shebeen every night, and always ran through his money by eleven. But he was proud, for such a thin sad man. So I lent him the money. He was a teacher at my old school, which means, not that Zanele would agree, he was our baba. Professor told me the money was important, which made me think this time it wasn't for umqombothi.

But I realized I shouldn't have lent the money, when Sizwe came to the shebeen to collect the earnings. I had expected him a week later, but still, it was stupid. Now, Sizwe sat opposite me on a barstool and licked his fingers as he counted what I handed to him from the locked drawer at the back of the bar. Mandla was with him, as usual. And this time, Lerato too. Sam stood at the other end of the room, pretending to adjust his tie, which looked like a stupid thing to do. If Sizwe guessed he was a police informant, and I was helping him, Lerato would moer both of us. I'd seen him do that too many times. Sizwe didn't like people having two jobs. Especially not jobs helping abo gata.

Sizwe didn't say anything as he counted. I could hear his fat fingers leafing through the notes. Mandla and Lerato waited, Mandla tapping his fingers against the counter.

Sizwe stopped counting and turned to him. "Mandla, stop doing that."

Mandla stopped. Sizwe counted again—even though we both knew the money was short. I offered him a whiskey. Sizwe looked up, said nothing.

Mandla began picking his teeth. He stopped and looked at me. "You have a problem, *umntwana*?"

"No problem, just looking at your nice teeth. So clean." Mandla leaned across the bar, and I stepped back, just a small step. Mandla had been angry ever since Sizwe had chosen me over him to run the shebeen.

Lerato watched us. He was getting irritated. I knew if I said anything else, he would throw me outside. Around here they called Lerato Sizwe's butcher.

I sat on the bartender's stool. Finally, Sizwe put the money in a white envelope and put it in his pocket. He got up from his chair. Lerato didn't move.

"You're short," Sizwe said, "by a hundred rand."

"Sorry, sir, I was expecting you next week, and I will have it by then."

"It's hundred less," he repeated.

"The police came in last week, on one of the big nights," I lied. "They took a hundred fifty. That's why."

Sizwe had been admiring the rings on his fat fingers, but now he looked at me. He nodded at Lerato, who picked me up until my feet were kicking against the counter. Mandla looked up at me and laughed.

"Thabo," Sizwe said, "I like you. You are a good boy. But I don't like excuses. I don't like lies. I don't want police in my shebeen, looking for mlungu. We have no fights with the police. And we never have mlungu. Understand?"

"I understand," I said. "Please, sir, I understand."

Lerato dropped me. For a few seconds I thought that was it. But then he hit me in the face. I got to my feet, fast. They left the shebeen, Lerato opening the car door for Sizwe. Mandla got in last.

The only way Sizwe could have known about the mlungu was if one of my people told him. "*Fok*," I said.

Through all this, Sam had been standing in the corner, watching. "*Voetsek*," I told him.

*Eish*, what did I expect from a boy who earned money off abo gata?


## Zanele

Mankwe and I sat next to each other on the stools against the wall, and ate *paap*. The wind blew cold clean air onto our faces. Mankwe had time before the show and hadn't dressed up yet.

"What are you going to sing today?" I asked her.

"Maybe some Thandi Klaasen or Mama Makeba."

"Which one?"

"Whatever Thabo says." She was looking past me to the open door.

"Whatever Thabo says?"

"He's the manager, Zani," Mankwe said. "And he's a good boy."

"Good boy that steals."

Mankwe looked at me. Her eyes were almost like mine,

almost. But larger. "Whatever he needs to do to get money."

She took out her face mirror, oval-shaped with a pink plastic frame and handle. It looked like a child's toy. Baba had found it in a rubbish dump years ago, and she'd kept it, along with a small picture of him that was tucked into the corner. The picture was old, Baba in a suit, hair pomaded, head back, microphone to his mouth. It had been taken at his brother's wedding, I think.

"Why do you still have that?"

Mankwe turned. "What?"

"You know what I'm talking about."

"He wasn't such a bad man, you know. People here respected him. When Thabo's gogo died, he made sure he kept his shack. Re-built the wall for him."

"Yes, that's what you always say."

She put a hand on my wrist. "Please, don't start arguing now. Don't fight me." Then she said, "One day soon I will leave, get married. Then it's just you and Mama."

"When are you planning to get married?" I said.

"Eish, Zani, I was just saying."

"And which man will you choose—bow tie Sam, Professor, Thabo or one of his friends?"

"Aye, Professor is not so bad."

"Professor?" I laughed. She started laughing too, almost like she didn't mean to. And I held on to her, laughing until we cried.

# SIX

## Jack

"MADAM, I AM SORRY, BUT CAN I GO HOME EARLY TODAY?" Lillian stood with her hands folded against her apron.

My mother looked up from her shopping list and lowered her reading glasses. "What for, Lillian? It's just past noon."

On the kitchen counter, past the living room, the vegetables stood chopped and ready on the board. Six stalks of asparagus sat in a glass.

"My daughter is sick, Madam."

"Your daughter is always sick, Lillian," my mother said, and turned back to her grocery list.

Lillian stood there, waiting. My mother didn't notice for a while, thinking that the conversation was over. Then she turned around. "No, I'm really sorry, Lillian, it's not possible. I need you for dinner tonight, and I know enough about those Putco buses you take to know that you won't be back on time. No, I'm sorry."

"Please, Madam, I won't take pay for today."

Mother folded her shopping list. "Now, Lillian, why would you say that? Just stay for dinner and leave afterward." My mother walked into the kitchen and checked the chopped vegetables.

"I'll drive you," I said. I didn't believe I'd offered until the words were out.

"No need, Jack." My mother's voice, incredulous, from the kitchen.

"No trouble," I continued. "I'll take you now and get you back by dinner. Have errands to run downtown anyway."

I was out the side door so quickly that mother didn't have a chance to argue.

Lillian was standing next to my car. I opened the door for her and she sat, putting her bag on her lap.

I took the highway, then Moroka Bypass, thinking of what I could say to start a conversation. Lillian had a wide face, wider than her daughter's—something about the set of her eyes and mouth fixed a serious expression on her face.

We said nothing. Again I took the left past the stadium, past some small broken brick houses, then over the township bridge.

The next thing I knew, I was turning and parking in front of the shebeen. It was the only place I knew here.

"Not here. Left," Lillian said.

Was she wondering—how does this white boy know the place where my daughter sings at night?

LILLIAN'S SHACK WAS MADE OF CEMENT BRICKS, AND WHERE the bricks had run out, corrugated metal of three different shades formed the wall and roof. Her place was in a line of maybe fifty of them, crammed next to each other for as far as I could see. The roofs of the shacks were low and cluttered with odd things—a barrel, a tire, rocks. A rusted green deckchair.

Through a hole in the metal I could see a small light.

Lillian opened the passenger-side door and stepped out, clutching her handbag. "Thank you, sir. I can take the bus back in time for dinner."

She shut the car door and walked into the shack. As she ducked inside, I realized she had a slight limp.

I got out of my car and walked up to the wall, crouching low until I came to the window, a hole cut clumsily in the metal with a piece of plastic taped over it.

Lillian was leaning over the bed and offering her daughter something from a plastic box. A different daughter, I realized, with a gentler, pale face. Then the singer entered the room and started talking to her mother, fastening the buttons on her sleeves. She walked out with a box in her hands and came up to my car. She stopped and looked in.

She turned, saw me, and walked up to me, grabbing my collar in exactly the same place as before. "What are you doing here?"

"Dropping your mother off."

There were flecks of yellow in her brown eyes. And her anger was as real as the first time I'd met her.

"You come to the shebeen, you insult me in your house and now you're looking in my window?"

"Mind letting go?"

"What?"

"My collar." I smiled.

She tightened her grip. "Leave my family alone. I don't care that you are playing some sick game. I have friends. They can make your life difficult."

"Do you mean the guy in the shebeen with the bad taste in hats?"

She smelled of soap and ironing, better than the perfume that time in the shebeen. Slowly she let go. I rubbed the spot where the starched ends of the shirt had cut into my neck.

"Yes, the tsotsi. Stay away." Her voice was different now, sort of bored. "Agh, now you've made me late."

She turned away, still holding the brown parcel, and walked between a gap in the shacks. I got into my car, started it, and followed her.

"Let me drive you to where you're going," I shouted through the window.

No response, not even a look.

"I'm sorry for the face paint, for—"

"Trying to pay me off? And you're not sorry. That's a lie."

"It's just a lift."

"Thank you, no. I do not want to be kidnapped by a mlungu." She stopped. "Unless—"

"Unless what?" I braked.

"You let me drive."

"Fine. You drive." What was I saying?

"I can?"

"Yes."

Without thinking too much about it, I slid over to the passenger seat. She got in the car, putting the parcel between us. She shut the door behind her and turned on the ignition. I watched her put the clutch in and put the car into gear. The car jerked forward, stopped suddenly.

"You don't know how to drive," I said.

"I'm learning," she said. "I learn fast."

"I think I should take over."

"No, that was the deal, I get to drive."

I took hold of the wheel. "Ease up on the clutch, slowly, and hit the accelerator, not too fast. This is a bad idea."

"Relax, mlungu. I've done this before. And I told you, I learn fast."

SOMEHOW WE GOT DOWNTOWN IN ONE PIECE. SHE HADN'T said anything else to me during the entire ride, so all I did was stare at her face. A wide forehead, sloping down to the nose, the mouth set in a firm line.

"What?"

"Nothing."

She pulled up to a curb, and we jerked to a stop by a shabby convenience store.

She turned the ignition off. The car whined down into complete silence. She pulled the hand brake and opened the car door. "See, mlungu?"

"It's Jack."

"I know," she said in a cold voice. "Jack Craven."

"What's your name?"

"You tell me."

"Zanele," I said. "Or at least that's what the men in the alley called you."

"When you came with your mlungu friends."

"Look, I know it was stupid."

"Is that what you thought when you did it? You can come to our shebeen, put black paint on your face and play a game?"

I didn't answer. I was getting to know that there was no point in apologizing again—not to someone like her.

Then she said, "Don't ever do that again, you and your friends."

"Okay," I said. It sounded like she wasn't going to tell my parents about the shebeen.

"If we'd caught you, we probably would have killed you." Her voice lacked expression. She stepped out on the road.

"You know the real reason why you don't like me?" I said. "I laughed at your singing."

"Don't be silly," she said. "Everyone from here to Orlando knows how bad my singing is." For a moment, it looked like she was laughing at me. But it was hard to tell.

She slammed the car door and walked off.

She'd left the parcel behind and I opened it. A mathematics book from last year's syllabus. And then, inside, a bunch of leaflets from banned organizations, the ANC, the PAC. Something about the Young African Religious Movement, meeting on 28th May. The car door clicked open again and the book was snatched away.

"That's mine," she said, with something like fear in her eyes.

I took the driver's seat, slipping the leaflet I'd taken into my pocket. I watched as her red-shirted figure disappeared down the street. Then I drove home.

I thought about the bad singing in the shebeen. Her hands

on the steering wheel. A silent mother with a limp. A calculus book filled with illegal politics that would send her to jail.

When I parked in front of my house and looked over the seat and dashboard, there was nothing to show she'd been here. But there was the leaflet, folded in the front pocket of my jeans.


# Meena

DURING THE AFTERNOON LULL, I SAW THE BLACK GIRL GET out of an old red Mustang that was parked at the corner of President Street. She was wearing a red shirt and carrying what looked like a brown postal package.

There was a guy in the passenger seat. He switched over to the driver's seat. He was white.

She walked quickly toward the shop.

I ran over and barred the door to the shop. If the plainclothes policeman in the car wanted to arrest me, he'd have to break the door first.

Now the black girl was on the other side of the door, pulling the book out of the postage parcel. When I didn't move to open the door, she started knocking on the glass. The car that had dropped her off reversed and was gone.

Slowly, I unbarred the door. "Took you long to open that door," the girl said. "This is yours." She held out the book.

I took it from her hands.

"You gave it to me."

"I don't know what you mean," I said.

"Where did you get all those pamphlets?"

"What were you doing with that policeman?"

"What police? . . . Oh." She smiled. I saw even white teeth. "That mlungu wouldn't know how to arrest someone if you gave him handcuffs and a gun. So," she said, pushing past me and walking into the store, "what were you doing with those pamphlets?"

"I like collecting them," I said.

"Collecting?" She laughed. "So you're not an ANC member, then?"

"No."

"Not an informer?"

"No. What kind of question is that?"

"Calm down. I didn't think so. You don't look like one. So then, what are you?"

"We have a new load of Ouma rusks in the store. You can have some, if you like," I suggested.

The girl raised an eyebrow. "Rusks?"

"Yes."

"What's your name?" she asked as she followed me to the counter.

"Meena."

"Okay, Meena. Don't keep those. You could get five years in jail for nothing." Her voice took on a tone I recognized, one I'd use on Jyoti or some small frightened animal.

I didn't reply, and put out the box of rusks. On the front, there was a hearty-looking white lady, holding out a batch from the oven. Her expression was bunched up, her face a bit like an Afrikaans pudding.

"What's your name?"

She opened the box, looked at me. "Zanele," she said.

Then I heard the bell that sounded every time someone entered.

The tsotsi had returned. Of course he would choose this time to come.

Very slowly, watching him the whole time, I moved toward the cash register. I opened the drawer—it made a grating, metal sound—and took out the kitchen knife I'd put under the ten-rand notes. I held it out so he could see it.

But the tsotsi wasn't looking at me at all. "Zanele," he said.

I'd forgotten how he looked, the broadness of his face and his jaw. It was hard to know how old he was. Today he wore black trousers, a red shirt, and suspenders with gleaming silver clips. The left side of his face was tender and swollen. His eyes moved slowly from Zanele to me, then to the knife. He smiled the way he had smiled before, when he had laughed at me.

"What are you doing?" Zanele asked, but I ignored her, concentrated on the tsotsi. His eyes flicked from Zanele to me. He took a step closer to me, the sole of his shoe squeaked against the floor. Another step, and his hand was over my grip on the knife.

Zanele came between us. "Give me the knife," she said, and held out her hand.

I tried to hand it over, but the tsotsi's hand was still tight around mine. So I jerked the knife in toward the tsotsi, putting my weight behind it. He was not expecting it. Zanele wasn't expecting it.

"Fok," he said. Blood spattered the floor. "*Fok, fok,*" he said.

I staggered back, still holding the knife, watching the way the drops made a crescent of small bumps on the linoleum.

"Drop the knife," Zanele said in an even voice.

I put it on the floor. Some of the blood had got onto my hand.

Zanele reached for the tsotsi's injured wrist, but he twisted away, closing his other hand over the cut. "Give a girl a knife, she starts stabbing everything." He took a yellow handkerchief from his pocket, then watched as more drops of blood fell onto the floor. He put the handkerchief back into his pocket.

Zanele took his wrist. "Your fault, you tried to take the knife from her." She turned to me. "Why did you do that? What has Thabo done to you?" Like the tsotsi, she didn't seem to be bothered by the cut.

"Thabo?" I said.

Zanele took the handkerchief from the tsotsi's pocket and pressed it onto the wound. They muttered something to each other in Zulu.

"Let me see the cut," I said. I took out our first aid kit from under the register.

"You crazy?" said the tsotsi.

"Give me your hand," I said.

"You heard me. No," the tsotsi said.

"We can stand here all day and watch, while you bleed all over the store," Zanele said.

"The store? You're worried about the store now?" The tsotsi's voice rose again.

"Let me bandage it," I said.

The tsotsi turned away from Zanele and looked at me. "Crazy," he said.

Zanele took the alcohol and the roll of bandages I was holding out. She was careless, but the job was good enough to keep the blood in, and the tsotsi didn't complain when she poured half the bottle of alcohol over his cut.

"You probably need three or four stitches," I said.

Zanele nodded, took his shoulder, and hurried him out of the store. They crossed President Street, heading for the closest bus rank. I know that there was no reason for me to see them again, so I locked the store and followed, standing behind them in the line to an old, battered Putco bus with the number 910 stamped across its dusty front. I found some coins to pay the chubby-fingered driver. His eyes on me were sharp, cold.

"Were you trying to steal from her?" Zanele asked the tsotsi.

"Yes, he was. Like he did last week," I said.

"You don't tell me what's stealing," he said, his voice flat.

Zanele made an impatient noise. "I don't want to hear about you going into that shop again, asking for money."

"Now you're friends with all the Indians you can find?"

A few women across the very narrow aisle moved their legs in so they wouldn't brush against the tsotsi. The rest of the people in the bus ignored us.

"Never again," Zanele said. "I mean it."

"We'll see about that," the tsotsi said.

Zanele grabbed his hat.

"Okay, okay," the tsotsi said, and took the hat from Zanele's fingers.

"That doesn't sound convincing to me," I said.

"Why is she here, anyway?"

"You're looking for money, aren't you?" Zanele said. "You're short for Sizwe, and he's going to set Lerato on you, isn't he?"

"No," the tsotsi replied sharply.

"I'll tell Mankwe you don't have to pay us for singing this week," Zanele said.

The tsotsi gave a soft, bitter laugh. "Zee, that's only five rand. I'm short by a hundred."

WHEN I STEPPED OUT OF THE BUS ONTO THE DIRT ROAD, I looked for familiar signs or landmarks, but there were none.

"This way," Zanele said. We followed her, took enough turnings that I was lost. Then I saw it. A tiny clinic with a battered sign. There was a line of people waiting for their turn in the winter sun.

"SHE STABBED ME." THE TSOTSI STEPPED INTO THE ROOM. He cocked his head at me to indicate who he meant.

"I did, but that's because he was stealing from us," I said.

"Not steal. Give me money you owe us, how many times do I have to say it?"

"We owe you nothing."

"You shouldn't have tried to take their money, Thabo," Zanele said. "And you, you don't know how to use a knife."

"It was meant as a deterrent."

The tsotsi scoffed. "Any fool can see you can't use the knife. Any fool."

"I got you, didn't I?"

"Let me see the cut," the doctor said, and stepped forward. He was a tall Indian man who stooped just slightly at the shoulders, but that was probably because of the low roof of the clinic. His coat was spotless white, and he, like everything else in the room, smelled strongly of disinfectant. A window in the corner let in a soft cool breeze. The doctor took a pair of scissors and undid the bandage slowly. He leaned forward and looked at the cut for a few seconds.

"I'm sorry, my boy. Stitches," he said.

The tsotsi turned to me. "Ja, now add that to your father's bill for me next week. Medical costs."

"How many times do I have to tell you, Papa doesn't owe you anything? Leave us alone. Leave our store alone."

The doctor watched us carefully, saying nothing. He turned to me, looking me over as he would a small child.

"What's your name?"

"Meena."

"Well, Meena, why don't you get that cotton wool over there, and the Dettol. I'm going to need your help, since my nurse is out."

I went over to the cupboard and found the bottle, as well as a plastic packet of wool.

"Not her," the tsotsi said.

The doctor ignored him. He took a sterilized needle from his kit and threaded it.

Zanele pinned Thabo's fingers on the table. The tsotsi was staring at her face.

I dabbed the wound. "It was a clean kitchen knife," I said to the doctor.

The doctor nodded, tying a small knot in his thread.

"Dankie. Baie dankie for using a clean knife," the tsotsi said.

The doctor's stitches were fine and precise. We watched in silence as he closed the cut I'd made. A few clean lines on the tsotsi's skin.

The tsotsi made a show of taking out his wallet, a fat leather thing with gold edges. "What do I owe you, doc?" he asked.

"Nothing this time," the doctor said, eyeing the wallet.

The tsotsi tried to say something, but the next people in line pushed past him.

"Can I come here again? To help?" I asked the doctor as he tossed his gloves in the sink.

The doctor smiled, tired. "Of course. But no more stabbing people, okay?"

OUTSIDE THE CLINIC, I SAW ZANELE LEADING THE TSOTSI away, their figures lost in the crowd. I took another Putco bus back to President Street. Everyone stared at me the whole ride. Then the few familiar steps back to the store.

Inside, my father was standing and looking at the blood. "What is this?" he asked.

SEVEN

## Thabo

I FOUND PROFESSOR'S BODY THE NEXT MORNING IN MY OLD school playground, next to the tire swing. His glasses were cracked and lay next to his face. Someone had stepped on them. Sangoma, the school cat, sat beside him.

I had heard them talking about Professor when I was walking up Mputhi Road this morning, looking for my money. There were some abantwana blocking my way and talking loudly. I picked one up. He knew who I was. "Where is the Professor?" I asked him.

"Please, Mr Thabo, I don't know."

"I heard you telling that girl a made-up story about him being killed."

WHEN I GOT TO THE SCHOOL, MY BOYS RAN AWAY. THEY WERE not used to looking at so much blood of people they knew. Even though they always told me they wanted to come with me on my real jobs. I brought some milk for Sangoma. He sat on my shoe and drank it. I looked at the body a while.

"He kept teaching maths in Afrikaans, even when we told him to stop," the boy told me. "That is why he is dead. They used a screwdriver."

The sound of car tires against the gravel in the road—the police. I bent down and checked Professor's pockets. Empty except for a few coins, and a receipt from a jewellery store. He'd found time to spend the hundred rand I'd lent him before he died—but not on umqombothi. I picked up Sangoma and walked away.

Anyway, Professor was just a drunk with too much school inside of him. He spent his spare time chasing after Mankwe, as if someone like her would look at him. There were hundreds of men like him all around here. I wasn't going to go around Soweto looking for a bloody screwdriver. It didn't matter which boys had done it. The police couldn't care less—a black boy killing a black man.

I was wrong about that, because then I heard a whistle, and I saw from the other side of the wire mesh that Sam Shenge, in a purple bow tie, was coming up. This would be a story for *The World* and something to report to the abo gata too. And Sam would tell the police the name of some poor *oke*, and the police would arrest him. Then Sam would get his full fee.

Sam pushed past the small gate and came up to where I was standing. I got a few punches to his face before he pushed me away. He wasn't going to look pretty tomorrow.

"Thabo, I didn't kill him. So why you hitting me?"

Behind him on the street, the abo gata were getting out of their car. I turned to leave.

"Why, Thabo?"

## Zanele

"Why did you get into that mlungu's car?" Mankwe sat on the chair, pulling up her stockings. Thabo had come by and told her she was still booked for tonight. Noon light shone through the window onto her bare legs and my arms. She had too much blush on her face. I didn't say anything. I just kept rubbing green soap against the blue cotton of Mama's uniform.

There was something strange about Mrs Craven's son. He changed every time I saw him, so that it was hard to know what kind of mlungu he was. The first time outside the shebeen, when I'd found him in black face, his leather jacket smelled of whisky and his voice had been loud. He hadn't been scared. Almost like he'd wanted to get caught. With me holding his shirt, he waited to see what I would do. And when he finally realized we were going to beat him, he ran away with his friends like it was a game.

Then the second time, at his parent's dinner table, he had been quiet, looking at his parents and guests like they were strangers. Everything about him was ironed and neat. His hair was combed carefully back and gleamed in the living room light. When anyone said anything, he agreed. Then he had come and offered me money to say nothing about being at the shebeen.

And then this last time when I drove his car. He stared and stared at me and didn't look away.

"Why?" Mankwe asked again.

"I don't know."

"Don't know? That's new."

"Anyway, it happened," I said. "We need to be careful with Mama working for that family."

"You need to tell her."

"I won't do it again."

I'm Jack, he'd said, as if his name would change everything. His friends and his mother. His giving money to keep people quiet.

"You're always finding new ways of getting arrested."

"That's not—"

"I know you better than anyone else. And yes, Zanele, that is what you do. You do not think about other people. You never have."

I took my hands out of the laundry bucket, carried it outside and threw the water out. Through the door, I could see Mankwe stepping into her heels. She picked up her mirror, smoothing the lipstick around the edges of her lips.

Then she put the mirror down and walked out to me and held my shoulders, her fingers pressing into my skin. "You haven't gone to school today," she said. "And you didn't go yesterday."

"Yes. I haven't."

"Zanele, all we want is for you to go to school and come back. That's all we ask."

"You sound like Mama. She told you that too. Now you go and put makeup on your face and sing at the shebeen like it's all you want from life. You keep doing the same thing over and over, thinking it will get you something better."

Mankwe's expression didn't change. She had to do the show in ten minutes. She wasn't going to mention Professor. "Yes, all of us except you, Zanele, are blind."

Then she left.

I finished hanging up the washing. I went back behind the curtain, to the part of the room that Mankwe and I shared. Her boxes of things had been tipped over and shaken out onto the floor. There was a pink gift bag with tissue paper coming out of it next to her mirror. I pulled out the tissue paper—a gold ring in box, and a letter written to Mankwe, written in sloped, looped writing that belonged to someone who found time to practise their handwriting—Professor.

I closed the letter and put it back so I wouldn't have to read it. Suddenly, I felt sick.

If things had been different, I would have teased her. "Why Professor? You can have anyone in Soweto. Why him?"

Now he was dead—a screwdriver in his chest. Killed by his students. Some of us.

As I waited for Vusi and the rest, I looked at the collection of cigarette butts on the ground outside school. There were layers of them—testament to so many meetings, so many plans made and rejected. It was May, and there was one more death to add to the list.

"Zanele," Vusi said. "Long time."

"Maybe not long enough," I said, as Themba ducked out of the bushes and dropped his cigarette. He was the tallest of the boys, a soccer player, not a debater. I stubbed out his cigarette with my shoe.

Themba smiled.

Masi pushed him out of the way and brushed the leaves off his bell-bottoms. "How's it?"

I looked up at him, trying to read his face, then Vusi's, then Themba's. I had not seen them for a few days. "I'm fine."

"You've heard," Masi said.

"Yes."

"This can't happen again," Masi said. "It can't. We need to make that clear tonight."

"How are you going to do that?" I asked. "How, exactly?" My voice was cold.

I took the path into the school, leading the way through a window into Mr Mamphile's classroom.

We pulled the chairs to the front and used lanterns to light up the desk. Just a few years ago, this classroom had belonged to one of Masi's heroes, Tiro, a history teacher and activist. He would walk around the classroom, shake his hands and shout about the Afrikaner, the Bantu system. They were such normal obvious things, but Tiro made us realize how the Boer did everything to make us hate ourselves, distrust each other.

Tiro went across the border to Botswana to get away from the abo gata. But we learned they sent him a parcel bomb. They say he died instantly. Masi talked about it sometimes.

We waited in silence for the others to come, from schools across Soweto.

"WE NEED TO TAKE THEIR FILTHY BUILDINGS, THEIR POLICE stations, their informants and burn them all." As Dlamini leaned closer, the lamp tipped forward. Masi grabbed it and moved it away.

We sat at a small wooden desk, our elbows touching, our faces a few inches apart from one other. The window looked out on the playground and the road, where cars bumped over the potholes at intervals. Vusi took notes.

"Hasn't today's killing been enough?" I said.

The others at the table stared at me. Vusi cleared his throat.

"Since when have you been the baas at this meeting?" one of the guys from Naledi said. I think his name was Winston. "I haven't even seen you here before."

"Professor was one of us, went to this school," I said.

"Zanele is right," Masi interrupted. "We cannot let this kind of thing happen again. We must work together. We have an objective: to establish cells in all the schools so that we can pass along messages within hours. A network that is undetectable by the police."

"That's magic, my friend," said Winston.

"We have Naledi. Even Orlando West. What about the others?"

"Phefeni," said Thandi. There was a scar on her face, from forehead to cheek.

"And I'm from Jabavu," said Dlamini.

"Who told you about our meeting?" asked Vusi.

"Zanele," said the boy.

"We are missing leaders from two schools, Zanele?"

"I told them about this meeting."

"Okay. Make sure they are here next time."

"We at Phefeni have news," Thandi interrupted. "We are planning our own strike."

"When, sisi?" Vusi asked.

"You will see," Thandi said.

"But don't you think, sisi, it would be better if we all worked together to make one strike?" Vusi asked, his voice gentle, persuasive. I knew that voice.

"When is your strike coming, bhuti? You have been telling us for weeks, and nothing has happened." Thandi leaned forward. The black-red of her scar glistened in the candlelight.

"Soon," said Masi.

"We are not waiting for your orders," Thandi said.

Vusi looked as if he was about to say something, but Masi put a hand on his arm. "It is good. More strikes are better."

"So next on the agenda. The school boycott," Vusi said.

We all heard it—a car slowing down, then stopping by the pothole, stopping at the school gate. Vusi's eyes moved to the window. A policeman got out, and then a blond man in a black suit. Wordlessly, Vusi crumpled his agenda and threw it to the other side of the classroom. Dlamini ran into the corridor. I didn't think he would get away before the police came.

"Masi can't be here," Themba said. "He can't."

"It's too late," Masi said, calm.

And it was, because the classroom door opened and the blond man came in. He looked familiar, I didn't know why.

"Good evening," he said, and walked slowly into the classroom. He came in alone.

There were twenty of us, but it would have been stupid for us to run out now. He walked to our table and stooped over. Where the lantern light caught his clothes, I saw they were dusty. He smelled of cigarettes.

He held out his hand to Masi, as if he knew who he was.

"Coetzee," he said. "Nice to finally meet you." The man's fingers were long, and he had rings on his middle and ring finger.

"Masi," Masi said, without taking his hand.

"I'm sorry to interrupt this . . ."

"Debate meeting."

"Debate meeting," Coetzee repeated, and smiled, the skin near his eyes and mouth cracking, as he looked around the silent classroom, its empty chairs, and the twenty of us clustered together. "Yes, very sorry, what is the debate?"

"We're debating," Masi said, "the tax system in the Bantustans."

"The tax systems? Interesting choice," he said, still smiling, walking around our table in a slow circle. His accent was mildly Afrikaans, and he spoke slowly, as if he liked to hear himself speak.

A policeman came in, holding Dlamini, whose shirt was torn, his arms twisted behind him.

"Ah, Coobus," Coetzee said to the policeman. "Why don't you let that gentleman have a seat?"

The policeman jerked the boy's arms apart and bent his body into a seat. The boy moved to get up—the policeman hit him on the side of the face, leaving behind a red line where the metal of his wedding ring had met skin. There was a gun in the policeman's belt. The boy looked away from us, but stopped moving.

"And I think, let's get rid of this table too," Coetzee said.

The policeman took the gun out of his holster and jerked it at Dlamini, who got up and moved the table away from us. I started helping him, and then Masi did the same. The policeman kept the gun on the boy until we were all in our seats, in a line, facing them.

"This is unpleasant. I know," Coetzee said. "But the reason I am here, as you may know, is that I'm looking for a young woman." None of us said anything. "Let me explain—"

"Excuse me, sir, but are you part of the police?" Masi asked. "Because I don't see a police badge."

The man laughed. "Let me explain," he said. "As I'm sure you all know, there were some trials a few weeks ago. Some people on this debate team, I believe, were arrested for terrorism. Now, they were very good at making sure they didn't implicate each other. Even after questioning. But, you see, I visited the guide at the power station the other day. Nice man. He remembers a boy, your friend Billy, and two girls. He's sure of it. And I wonder if you people know of this other girl that the guide was referring to?"

He looked up and down, lingering on each of our faces. And then he stopped and stooped over Thandi, and looked at her wide scar. She did not blink. Her chest rose and fell slowly, like she was sleeping.

Then he came to Tina, who was from Naledi. He looked at her small pretty face. Then finally, he came to me. I saw that his skin on his face was spotted pink, brown and white. Maybe someone had poured something hot on him and left it there, for a long time.

"What is your name?"

"Zanele," I said. I forced my palms to be still in my lap. I hadn't given my name to the guide at the power station. This man could not know for sure that I had been at the power station, unless Billy or Phelele had told. But Billy had come back changed. He didn't even want to speak to me now.

"You're a singer at one of the local shebeens, I'm told. Very good."

I said nothing.

"You don't know who it was at the power station, Zanele?"

"No, I don't."

Coetzee finally straightened, smiled. "Then we both don't know. Isn't that strange? But I'm sure the guide will be able to tell us. Don't you think so, Zanele, that he will be able to tell with a picture?"

"You've said so," I said, keeping my voice even as the shock of him saying my name went through me.

"But you don't think so. He doesn't seem reliable to you?"

"It would be a pity if he identified the wrong person."

"I agree. But if you find out who she was, you will let me know, won't you?" Coetzee said. "Oh, I completely understand.

You won't want to tattle on your friends." He took a cigarette from his pocket. "Come Coobus, I think we can go, as long as these young people know who we are looking for. But I also hope they tell this friend of theirs that if she is caught with some of her other friends trying to cross the border, the police have no responsibility to ensure their safety."

The policeman slowly put the gun back in his holster. None of us moved.

"It's the cleanest way for us to do our job here, waiting for criminals at the border," Coetzee said. "No paperwork. No explanations." Then he walked out of the room. Coobus followed.

It took a while for the sound of their footsteps to fade out. Dlamini finally brought his hand to his bruised face.

"I don't understand," Masi said.

Vusi put covers over the lanterns and pushed out our chairs, folding them back in the way they'd been. "He'll wait for one of us to try to cross the border with Zanele."

"He could have arrested her now," Masi said.

"He's not sure it was her. He was guessing," Vusi said. "He doesn't want just one person, he wants us all, including the ones in SASO."

"But what about our Baas education plans? We were all together, and he didn't even try and question us about it."

"Think about it, Masi. Underground cells with weapons, planning to blow things up," I said. "And a bunch of school kids protesting some education law—what would you pick to investigate?"

"He is making a mistake," Masi said quietly.

The rest of us didn't say anything. We put out the lanterns and carried them home.

# Jack

"Your mom hates me." Megan put a grape in her mouth and looked at me. Her dark, almost-black hair was in a neat bun.

"I hate my dad's beer, rainy days and cheap whisky. We all have our preferences."

"Thanks for that."

"Anytime. It's called Trident. Doesn't make any marketing sense, and he refuses to admit it." I put my hand over my eyes to shade them, and leaned back.

"I'm getting restless, you know? Living like this, it's getting under my skin."

When we'd first met, near the end of last year at a party at St John's College, she'd said something similar about going to Roedean's Girl School, wearing those brown stockings and sitting in the wooden chapel every day. That night, we'd gone home together. It was a good pick-up line.

"At least you're going away," she said. "You have a new place to get to know. New people to meet."

"You can go abroad too."

"Don't talk about things that aren't going to happen."

Megan was studying English at Wits, and spent the rest of the time being part of organizations like NUSAS. My mother thought NUSAS was "radicalized," but I'd been to a meeting once with Megan. It was just a bunch of thin, tame guys with long hair, arguing in low boring voices. I left the meeting early to fit in a game of tennis with Oliver.

"Become a journalist, like your dad," I said. "You like annoying people like the Van Roonens."

"Is this a dig at me for showing them for the narrow-minded uneducated racists they are?"

"No," I said. "I just wonder what you think we are, you and I. Educated racists?" I drank my glass of water and felt my headache ease a little.

"We don't want to be racist."

"Really?"

"That's the problem with you, Jack. I'll say you're a racist, you'll agree, then go back to whatever you like doing in your spare time, hanging out with Oliver and Ricky, driving your car all over the place. You're apolitical. No one can hate you for that, you don't allow them to."

"Best compliment you've ever given me."

"Right."

Lillian came in and set up the ironing table on the porch. Every time she entered the room now, I noticed her, expected her to say something. She couldn't know her daughter had driven my car downtown.

We got up from the table. Megan leaned in and kissed me. Her lips brushed my two-day-old stubble. I needed to shave. "Take me to lunch," she said.

Lillian was ironing the shirt with the mended collar. The stitches only showed if you were really close.

We passed through the living room to the front door. We got in the car, and as we drove to the Inanda club, I thought of Lillian's daughter, darker than her mother, skin that covered smaller, sharper bones. Her shifting moods, the way her face changed when she forgot she was talking to me. A showgirl laugh she'd picked up from goodness knows where.

I should have forgotten about her. But I couldn't.


# Meena

ON THE WAY TO THE CLINIC, PAPA WAS SILENT. I SAT NEXT TO him in the passenger seat, staring at Mama's lucky snowman dangling from the rear-view mirror, jumping with every pothole we went over. She would be pointing, telling Jyoti and I to look at the dirt streets, the mothers in their colourful skirts and their babies bundled tightly to their backs.

Papa parked the car in front of the faded LOWER JABAVU WESTERN CLINIC sign, and waited. Outside, there was no line of people. It was early, only eight on a Saturday.

Dr A. came, holding a long overcoat, carrying a briefcase covered in children's stickers. When he saw me step out of the car, followed by my father, he nodded. Wordlessly, he unlocked the door to the clinic. Papa stared—a real Indian man working in the township.

Papa stared at the photographs on the wall. "You play cricket?" he asked.

"Yes," Dr A. answered, taking a white coat from a hook. He waited politely for Papa to say something more. But Papa, always quiet with strangers, had become even quieter since Mama died. He just smiled, hesitating. Then he made a sort of bow, and left.

"Why don't you get a clean pair of gloves from that shelf," Dr A. said.

AROUND MIDDAY A YOUNG WOMAN WALKED IN, WEARING AN orange dress with flares at the bottom, and small shiny flower-shaped earrings. She had put on fake eyelashes. Not that she needed them. Anyone could see that. Behind the layer of blush, her skin was strangely pale.

"Mankwe," Dr A. said, "I didn't expect you."

She opened and closed her handbag, a cheap, shiny brown thing. "I came to check if you had some of those supplements."

"You passed out again?"

She didn't answer.

"Your sister and mother know?"

"No."

"You shouldn't have gone to sing," Dr A. said. "I told you."

Mankwe lowered her eyes, looking for something in her handbag. Then she said in a quiet voice, "I wake up every day and I don't want to leave the bed, do anything. My mother, every morning, goes to Houghton to clean. My sister goes to school and takes care of me, sings for me all those nights I can't make it. And she hates it. Why should a girl still in school have to sing in the shebeen?" Mankwe looked up. "So I go and sing. It doesn't matter."

Her eyes moved slowly from the doctor to me. The resemblance was so strong—except for her voice. Mankwe's was softer, nicer than Zanele's.

"Zanele," I said. "She's your sister?"

"Who is she?" Mankwe asked Dr A.

"She's helping," he said.

"How do you know my sister?"

"I'm her friend."

"Zanele never said anything about you."

"Maybe she doesn't tell you everything," I said.

"Don't talk about things you don't know."

"Mankwe. Supplements." Dr A. handed her a bottle. "It's the last one we have."

"Thank you. Thank you." Mankwe hugged him.

Dr A. was so much taller than her, it looked like he was hugging a child. Mankwe opened her handbag and held out some money. "See? I did a show every night this week, and so I can pay. Here."

He took the change and put it on his desk. She smiled. Then she left.

Dr A. rearranged his medicine cabinet.

"So she's anaemic?" I asked.

"Yes. Severely," he said.

I stared at the change. "But can't anaemia be helped with a good diet? Chicken livers, dates, spinach?"

"Meena," he said, "that girl's fiancée was just stabbed to

death with a screwdriver. She's lucky if she wakes up and finds some paap and can convince herself to eat it. And you know something about mealie meal? It doesn't have any iron at all."

## EIGHT

## Zanele

I DUCKED UNDER THE ROOF AND SKIRTED AROUND THE BACK. The only thing I could hear were the sounds of cars coming and going, their tires through the puddles of water on the side of the road.

"You're late." Meena stepped out from under Starlight Cinema's awning, wearing a black woolen coat and her school shoes.

"I know."

"You've seen this?" Meena pushed a copy of *The World* toward me. I tipped the paper under the streetlight: ANTI-AFRIKAANS PUPILS GO ON STRIKE IN SOWETO.

"It was Phefeni," she said. "They threatened to beat up the headmaster. Cut his tires."

"I know."

At the corner of the picture, behind all the children, I saw Thandi, her fist raised. I handed the paper back and started walking, keeping close to the sides of the building.

"They didn't agree to their demands though," Meena said.

"Shhh," I said. I imagined her putting pillows in her bed and sneaking out. She was young. If she was seen with me now, that Special Branch policeman Coetzee would be after her too.

I cut in front of Meena and upped the pace.

"You're too worried," Meena whispered, catching up to me. "It's an open meeting for the Young African Religious Movement. That's what the police think."

"You think they're that stupid?"

I pressed her back against the shadow of the storefront as a police car came driving by. It passed and we walked on, heels clapping against the pavement. She didn't say anything else.

INSIDE, IT WAS BRIGHTLY LIT. I PUT MY BACK AGAINST THE wall, scanning the room as Meena took off her beanie and scarf. People stared back at me, muttering. For half of them, I was the tsotsi's girlfriend, and for the others, I was the girl in the front row of the classroom all through standard five, six and seven.

Vusi walked over to me. "Good to see you," he said. I could see he was irritated I was there with this Indian girl.

"You too, Vusi."

Vusi turned to stare at Meena.

"I saw you at the SASO meeting last week," Meena said. "You're one of their masterminds, aren't you?"

"And who are you?"

"What happened to that school teacher? Stabbed in his own schoolyard."

Vusi stepped closer. It was a lazy step, almost as if he didn't mean it. "Sorry, I don't understand. Why are you here?"

"Same reason as you," Meena said.

"Watch it," Vusi said, an edge to his voice. Then he walked away.

"Meena, what was that?" I said.

"He didn't like me mentioning the stabbing, did you see that?"

"I knew that man. And my sister knew him too."

"Sorry," Meena said. "I didn't know."

"If I knew you came here to fight with people, I'd have left you back home."

By now a group of people were standing at the front of the hall, and four men entered from the side door. People stopped talking.

The four men took off their hats and coats. The banned PAC leaders.

Meena's face lit up as they talked about freedom, about resistance and hope. Meena didn't get it—all those PAC men did was give advice. People like Billy, Vusi and I were the ones who took risks.

## Jack

OLIVER'S DAD LEANED OVER AND HELPED HIMSELF TO MORE meat. In the candlelight, folds of white fat showed through the pink. Superintendent Joubert liked his meat rare. Next to me, Oliver was turning the knife over and over in his hand, watching his father eat. The dinner had already stretched past an hour. I was going to be late.

"What I don't get, Anna," Joubert said to my mother, after taking another bite of meat, "is why you won't tell the boy to get his education here. We have good schools."

My mom laughed politely and nibbled on a bean. My father walked in, hung up his coat and wiped his hands on a napkin. My mother's eyes lingered on his dirty fingers.

"Because, Jacques, she wants him to grow up an English gentleman. And South Africa's not the place for that." My father smiled, tired. He was returning from another failed Trident sales pitch.

Joubert snorted.

My mother finished chewing and gave my father a warning look.

"You see, that is your problem. You people aren't used to fighting. Always trying to get out of conscription. This country isn't for English gentlemen, we showed you that, we drove you out in the end."

"I served my time, Joubert. Angola," my father said, as he took his seat and put a napkin over his lap. "So don't be cross with me. I paid my dues."

If you looked closely at my father's face, you could see where the bullet had grazed him. The skin was a different colour there. It was whiter, stretched out.

Joubert turned to me. "Ah, you people must be so happy that Angola is done. This boy will never have to know how to hold a gun."

Oliver stopped eating and waited for me to say something. I smiled back.

"My son was captain of the rugby team, if you remember." There was a controlled note in my mother's voice. Of course, a reminder of how I'd made it to captain while Oliver was only a reserve. "And he hunts with his father. He's more than capable of handling a gun."

"Thanks, Mother," I said. I turned to Joubert. "I heard there's been some unrest lately in the townships."

Oliver coughed, clearing his throat.

"Had a meeting with your friend Van Roonen to get my beer into the Bantustans and to Soweto," my dad said to Joubert. "He gave the excuse that the political climate is inopportune, not only in the townships, but over there too. What with Transkei getting independence and all."

"Ja well, we'll see. I've got my men out in the townships, and I guarantee it's nothing, just a few black kids making noise. Easy to find them and lock them up."

"Just a few?" I asked.

Joubert chewed and swallowed a piece of steak.

"Jack has got a theory of how to control the townships, Joubert. I think it's pretty interesting." My father leaned back and took out his cigars.

I had no theory.

"Interesting?" Joubert said.

"It's a matter of research," I said. "I believe it's possible to predict the size of a protest based on the prevailing mood in the townships."

Joubert grunted.

"Take past incidents, for example. You record where the most serious incidents of unrest have happened, and when, and how frequently. Then you plot a trend line to predict township unrest. A parameter for where an incident is most likely to happen. When it's going to happen. And how big it's going to be. From that, a very rough model can be developed for policing more efficiently and effectively."

Joubert took a cigar from the case my father offered and let my father light it. "Interesting." He put the cigar in his mouth and leaned back. "I'll give you this, John, your boy is not stupid." He rolled the cigar around in his fingers before taking a long drag. "But he doesn't realize how irrational the black man is. But maybe Coetzee would be interested in talking to this boy." He paused, hesitating. "He likes these kinds of theories. And he is in charge of the intelligence coming out of Soweto."

I WOULD FIND OUT MORE ABOUT COETZEE LATER, FROM Oliver. But back then I didn't pay much attention to the story or the mention of the man. Oliver had met him once at dinner with his father. Coetzee told them over dessert how his parents had been murdered, and had chuckled afterward. When Coetzee was seven or eight years old, the gardener had set the house on fire with his family inside. Oliver was impressed by the fact that he was fluent in Zulu and Xhosa. Months later, I would imagine Coetzee as a child, with the gardener leaning down and telling him all about the flowers and birds.

A COUPLE MINUTES LATER, I WAS DRIVING AWAY FROM JOUBERT, Oliver, the dinner, having lied to my mother, my father, Oliver and his father. Lies had to be finely balanced, a mixture of detail and vagueness. This time I said I was going to see a friend, maybe catch the late night show. They all thought I was going to spend the night at Megan's, but didn't want to say so.

That night at the shebeen came vividly to mind—Zanele's glittering red dress against the inky black night, leading the mob of men and children. The shards of glass as the headlight smashed. And the firm set of her lips in profile against my car window.

I SLOWED THE CAR AND STOPPED TO CHECK IF I'D GOT THE address right. Then I saw a stream of people running past the car. It looked like the meeting was over. Students were running from the building, ducking under cars and yelling. It was worse than that time at the shebeen, and somewhere in the middle of this would be Zanele.

## Zanele

I SAW VUSI'S FIGURE AHEAD OF ME AS WE RAN. I WENT IN A different direction so we wouldn't be caught together. I held on to Meena too, which slowed me. As we rounded the corner we came slap into a policeman.

Behind him, his car flashed green and yellow.

"Passbook," he said. His uniform looked tight and new on him.

I did nothing. If I took my passbook out, it would show I didn't have a stamp for today.

"I said, passbook."

"Do it," Meena whispered, her eyes fixed on the policeman's chest.

I reached inside my shirt and pulled out the passbook. The policeman stared. His head was too large and round for the rest of his body.

He took his time to open it and page through it.

"You're not supposed to be here," he said. "Both of you. What were you doing here? Get in the car."

I turned to look behind me, at the empty road. No one would know if we disappeared.

"Not having the correct details in the passbook is a fine, not an arrest," Meena interrupted. "That's the law."

"Get in the car," the man repeated.

"No," I said.

"What did you say?" The man leaned forward, his eyes waiting. Just waiting.

"I said no," I repeated. I knew I'd regret it. The policeman closed his hand around my arm. It was clammy, the fingers thin and powerful. He could take us wherever he wanted.

Suddenly, there was a voice, and a car came into view. A red, shabby Mustang with the front light still broken. Jack Craven leaned out of the window and waved. "Zanele, my mother's been expecting you three hours ago," he said. He looked from me to Meena, then finally to the policeman.

The man's hand pressed into my skin.

Jack stepped out of the car. He walked slowly over to the policeman until he was close enough to lean forward and read the name on his badge. "Officer Lourie?" Jack said.

"Who are you?" said the policeman.

"Jack Craven," he said, like it was meant to mean something. He held out his hand.

I was between a spoiled white boy and a policeman, and I had to be quiet while they fought over me.

Jack sent me a careful warning glance. Like we'd done this many times.

"Come, Lourie. I would hate having to drag Superintendent

Joubert all the way here to sort out this mess. Just left off having dinner with him now. Our place is a mess because the two of them are late." Jack had a smile fixed on his face.

The policeman hesitated, let go.

Jack cocked his head in the direction of the car and turned back to the policeman. We walked over to the car. If we rushed, we'd give it away.

"Here, here's my driving license." Jack handed it to the policeman as if he were doing him a favour. "I completely understand, you must take my details."

"I'm going to check on you, hey," the policeman said.

"Please do," Jack said.

Meena closed the car door. "How do you know this guy?"

"My mother cleans his house. That's it."

Jack turned back to the car, still smiling, hands in pockets. Then he got in, gave the policeman another wave, and started the car.

The police car followed. I watched it drive out of sight.

"Stop the car," I said.

"I just got you out of an arrest," Jack said.

"Stop the car."

"That policeman was itching to break your wrist right there."

"Stop the car."

"Don't be silly," he replied, looking at me in the rear-view mirror. "I'll drive you back home."

Jack took a sharp left, toward Parktown, or maybe Soweto.

"I don't believe we've met before," he said, glancing at Meena in the mirror. "I'm Jack."

There he was again. Making friends.

"He was the white guy who dropped you at the shop that time, wasn't he?" Meena said.

I didn't answer.

"I'm trying to help you. You should know that by now." He

braked. "If you want to leave, leave. Or I'll drive you home. Last time you were in here you didn't seem to mind so much."

"I think we should let him take us away from here," Meena said. "Drop us at Pillay's All Purpose, on President Street, please."

Jack started the car up again. He smiled at me in the rear-view mirror. I didn't smile back.

NINE

# Jack

I LOOKED AT ZANELE IN THE MIRROR. SHE WAS SITTING IN THE back seat next to her friend, an oversized, ugly blue jacket around her shoulders. Her hands were folded on her lap. When she sensed I was looking at her, she raised her eyes to meet mine in the mirror.

"So, how was the meeting?" I asked.

She didn't reply.

"Fine," the Indian girl said.

"What was the meeting about?" I asked, another question directed at Zanele. "There are so many things people protest about these days, I lose track."

"How did you know there was a meeting?" the Indian girl asked me.

Zanele shot her a look.

"I read it," I said. "From your friend's collection."

"He read it?" her voice rose, panicked.

"I'm not going to turn you in. Don't worry."

"How can we be sure?"

"I just got you out of that policeman situation."

"That could have been staged," the Indian girl said.

"You have a vivid imagination."

She smiled.

"So what was that meeting about?" I asked again. "To get our friend Lourie so excited?"

"You tell me," Zanele replied.

Up ahead, President Street was in sight, her friend's stop. They opened the doors, got out.

I took the long way home. For some reason, I wanted the shebeen singer to trust me.

Chasing your maid's daughter. A fine game, Jackie boy, Ricky would say if he knew.

When I got home, I poured myself a drink on the porch. There had been something satisfying about playing around with the Lourie guy.

I MET MEGAN FOR LUNCH AT THE GOLF COURSE THE NEXT DAY.

"The township's on edge because of the new Afrikaans law."

"Afrikaans?"

"They're making all the children there switch from English to Afrikaans."

"So that's it?"

"Why all these questions, Jack?" She laughed. "You thinking about joining in?" She put on her cardigan and walked ahead of me, out of the restaurant and onto the golf course.

It was a crisp winter afternoon. The aloes had opened in streaks of orange in the flower bed next to the outside tables.

I used to like the way Megan laughed at me. I liked Megan, that was it. Back then there was no one else—and there was no reason not to take Megan to parties, to dinner, to weekends in Cape Town.


# Meena

THERE WAS A REASON WHY SCREWDRIVERS WEREN'T THE BEST tool for cutting through to the heart. The tip was wide and blunt, forcing a slow entry into the rubbery fibres and fascia of the pectoral muscle over the heart.

The teacher in Soweto was stabbed five times—twice in the stomach, two superficial cuts on the chest, then the puncture of the heart.

None of the newspapers—*The Drum, The World, Rand Daily Mail* or *The Times*—mentioned in what order the wounds were made. Maybe whoever stabbed him didn't know they were going to kill him. Maybe.

That guy at the PAC meeting had been annoyed when I'd brought up the murder. Zanele hadn't been pleased either when I mentioned it. She said she knew the teacher, and what she really meant was that it was none of my business.

I took the newspapers with articles about the stabbing down from the shelf to read them again.

That's when the white boy came in, the one from two nights ago. He walked straight to the counter and waited for me, staring at the chewing gum next to the register.

I saw now that he was one of those rugby tennis types from all-boys white schools like St Stithians or Jeppes. His eyes were cold.

"Can I help you?" I said.

"We met a few nights ago. I'm Jack. You're—sorry, I'm terrible with names." He held out his hand.

The shop bell rang.

And the tsotsi walked in, this time wearing a black army-style beret.

"I'm sorry," I said to the white guy, "I—"

"We've met," the white boy said, an edge of impatience coming into his voice. "We have."

The tsotsi picked up a magazine and paged through it, looking at us. His eyes were small, deep-set in his face. The beret gave him an even meaner look.

Zanele had told him not to come back, but here he was, waiting for the white boy to leave.

And then slowly, almost without realizing it, I slid my gaze from the tsotsi to the white boy. The tsotsi wanted money? Well there it was, in the white boy's back pocket.

"Yes, okay," I said to the white boy. "I know. So what kind do you want? Chappies?"

The tsotsi kept paging through *Huisgenoot*, waiting. For God's sake.

The white boy smiled, like I'd said something funny. He reached into the plastic jar and took out a handful and dropped them on the counter. Then he took out another handful, and another.

The tsotsi put down the magazine, walked up to the counter next to the white boy and stared at the pile of Chappies. He slid over a tube of toothpaste and a coin.

"Really? Toothpaste?"

"Thula wena," he answered.

I handed over his change. The tsotsi took the toothpaste and left without a word. He must have taken the white boy's wallet while I picked out his change.

I smiled. "You want that many Chappies?"

"Not really."

I picked up the newspaper and started reading.

"You're one of those liberal types," he said. "*Rand Daily*."

"So what?"

"Nothing. A friend of mine—her dad's the editor."

"Okay." I continued reading.

"You know Zanele pretty well, right?"

As if I didn't know the whole time that was why he'd come to the shop. The other night he'd stared at her in the rear-view mirror like there was no tomorrow.

"Who's Zanele?" I said.

"Come on," he said. He leaned his elbow on the counter and waited. "I'd like you to pass on a message to her."

"What is it?"

"Tell her to call me." He tore off a piece of the newspaper, scribbled a number and passed it to me.

"Why don't you pass on the message yourself?" I said,

taking the piece of paper. "Avalon cemetery."

"What?"

"Cemeteries usually have funerals," I said, sliding over the obituary from *The World*. As he read it, I counted the Chappies and put them in a bag.

"Thanks for this," he said, taking the newspaper and the bag of Chappies. "How much?"

"Seven cents."

He dug into his back pocket. Frowned. "I could have sworn I . . ."

"On the house this time," I said.

"I'll pay you later," he said. Still frowning.

"Sure," I said.

He looked back once before leaving the shop. We knew he was about to do something he wasn't supposed to do. That there were going to be consequences. And I was helping him.

## Jack

"I'M THINKING, FOR THE HORS D'OEUVRES, GREEN OLIVES ON toothpicks, and some of that smoked cheese Dad picked up from that shop in Parktown. No, no, that's too simple for a farewell party." My mother leaned back in her chair. "How about some Italian truffle cheese on a cracker. And then a sprinkling of caviar?"

I sat at the other end of the table, playing with my car keys. Lillian stood behind my mother's chair.

I wondered whether Zanele would be called in to help.

Lillian's hands were crossed over her apron, her eyes on the back of my mother's chair.

"I'll get what's on this list, and we'll just stick with that." I took it from my mother and put it in my new wallet. "Anything you make will be great, Mom. Oliver, Ricky and the rest will love it. I don't want you to stress about it."

"It's your last party, Jack. I want it to be perfect."

"Sounds like a death sentence," I said under my breath as I left the room.

I GOT OUT OF THE CAR AND SAW A LINE OF POLICE CARS PARKED against the curb across the street. What they were doing at a funeral, I couldn't say.

She was standing apart from the funeral procession, watching it. She was wearing that oversized blue jacket again, and carrying a large plastic Pick'nPay bag. Her arms were crossed, and her eyes followed the coffin's progress through the crowd. The going was slow. There was a lot of shouting and singing.

"You're not wearing black."

Zanele looked at me, then turned back to the procession. She didn't look surprised to see me.

All around us were swathes of open green-yellow land waiting for people to be buried. We watched as the casket was lowered into the ground. A tall woman leaned forward and threw in the first handful of dirt. The soil was dark, almost black.

Slowly, people dispersed except for a small cluster gathered around the grave—the tall woman, who was crying loudly, and two older women, holding her.

Zanele exhaled slowly, her eyes fixed on the stragglers.

"I think—"

"Be quiet, mlungu."

"I see police cars," I said, pointing at them.

I turned around and started to walk back to my car. I sensed her following me—but I didn't look back to check. I knew not to.

Her hand caught the handle of the passenger door, and

opened it. She got inside, silently. "Start the car," she said, tapping me, her fingers on my arm, like we'd known each other a long time. "The police are waiting."

I reversed, putting the car into a fast turn, and then straight along the dirt track that curved away from the cemetery. Through the rear mirror, I watched the police cars. It didn't look like they moved.

I turned into Moroka Bypass and took the right lane.

"Stay left. And when you come to the next light, turn right."

"Where are we going?"

"You'll see, mlungu. Be patient. You're the one who follows me everywhere I go, now I'm letting you to drive me around."

WE STOPPED IN FRONT OF A SMALL UGLY BUILDING.

"What's this?" I said.

"A school."

"It's Saturday."

"I know what day of the week it is." She picked up her plastic bag. She opened the door, scanning the road and the building.

I took the key out of the car, shut the passenger door and followed.

When I walked inside the school, I saw she was scattering paper all over the dark smelly corridor.

I leaned down and picked up one of the sheets. "They're just announcements. A debate. Nothing else."

"Disappointed?"

"What's the point of this?" I asked her, still lingering the paper.

"You tell me," she said.

"How would I know?"

She didn't reply. I stood there as the sheets of paper fell around me. Then I walked around and looked into the classrooms, with their crowded, lopsided seats. The sums on the blackboard were written in an unsteady hand.

"I'm done," she said. She walked ahead of me to the car, saying nothing.

"How many schools are you going to do?"

"Are you bored already?" she asked. "You're the one who volunteered."

"I don't get the point of it."

"It's better you don't."

"You knew I was coming. Meena must have told you. You brought this stuff along and planned to use me as your driver."

"Is that what you think is happening?" She smiled.

We got back in the car.

At the seventh school, I got the feeling that we were being followed. I didn't say anything for a while. But when we were about to turn onto the school grounds, I made a sharp right, away.

"What are you doing?"

"We're being followed."

The police car matched our pace.

# Zanele

We'd turned onto a small street, the car scraping against the shack walls. Jack's eyes flicked from the rear-view mirror to the turning ahead. Then he turned left, out onto the road that led to the highway to Wynberg. The car behind us was closer now.

"Hold tight," Jack said. He turned sharply, onto the island. The car swerved for one awful moment, and the tires scraped and shuddered as we went over. I heard swearing and honking, but now we were on the highway, heading in the opposite direction. Jack took the exit and accelerated.

He leaned back in his seat, taking one hand off the steering wheel. There was no sign of the police car.

"You're proud of yourself, aren't you?" I said.

He smiled, said nothing.

Ahead, the view changed, from buildings to houses to *koppies*, to flat, empty land and short trees.

"YOU KNOW THIS PLACE?" HE ASKED. HE STOPPED, PULLING the handbrake.

"My friend borrows a car sometimes." All around us, the land rose. The veld grass was yellow and long. From the road, we couldn't be seen. He opened the car door and got out. He looked up and smiled, his hands in his pockets.

He looked calm, like he was in the habit of running from police.

I stayed in the car, watching the mlungu.

That whole night after he'd dropped Meena and me at the store, I stayed awake, sure that Mama would get fired in the morning, and the police would show up with handcuffs at our shack.

He came to the window on my side. Close. His eyes were an unclear, watery colour, grey or black or blue, and there was something in them that was laughing at me. But the rest of his face looked like it belonged to an honest person. Someone you wanted to trust. The mlungu had looked like that when he'd come the first time to drop Mama at home, saying he was sorry for painting his face black. But I didn't believe him. And he knew it too. Still he tried.

"Coming outside, for fresh air? They say it's good for the nerves."

"I'm fine. Maybe you are the nervous one. It's hard for mlungus to run away from the police."

"It is hard, I agree," he said.

He looked up at the sky, squinting. His collared sleet-grey shirt blew out in the wind. He looked thin, but I knew he could run fast. The way he had looked at that policeman last night. Like it would be no problem to cuff the policeman and send him back in his own car. How little he knew.

"So, your friend," he said. "He drives you here?"

"That's none of your business," I said.

He stared at me, then smiled at me like we were sharing a joke. "True."

THAT NIGHT I FELL ASLEEP, DREAMING OF THE YELLOW STALKS of grass and gravestones, but not of the mlungu.

## Meena

IT LOOKED LIKE PILLAY'S ALL PURPOSE HAD ADDED TO ITS list of loyal customers, because the black car came again. This time without passengers. The man with the spotted rash was back. He walked in with that same strange, loose-limbed walk.

"Sisi," he said, "how are you?"

"Lucky Strikes?" I said, trying to sound friendly. I went over to the shelf and got two packs.

"This time one," Jonas said.

"Your baas didn't come with you?"

"He came," the man said. "But I drop him there in the township."

I handed over the Lucky Strikes.

"He is a good man, my baas. He works hard."

"For the police?"

"Yes," said Jonas. "There's trouble in the township, people fighting with the government, trying to blow up buildings."

Jonas shook his head. "It's too much, they must just stop."

"You like working for the police?"

"My baas, he is a very good man," Jonas said, looking past me at the cigarette packs. I stared at his rash again, wondering what it was. "He gave me this job. This is the best job. He buys me food and a nice place to live. He took me out of the mines. Have you seen the mines?"

"No," I said.

"When he was small, my baas," Jonas said, lowering his voice, "he was burnt in his own house by the gardener. His mother, his father, his sister, they died."

"That sounds—"

"Even then, even then he helps a black man like me. Takes me away from the mines, gives me clothes."

"I see."

TEN

# Zanele

IT WAS FIVE O'CLOCK AND DARK INSIDE, BUT LIGHT ENOUGH TO see the curved metal outline of the shacks opposite, the washing lines against the sky. I poured the pot of water I had been heating on the stove into the bath, and stepped in, resting my back against its sloping metal sides.

The mlungu spoke calmly. He seemed to like me, but he seemed to like everybody. He smiled often, talking as if we had known each other a long time. He had lied to the police casually, like he'd done it many times before. Even if I ignored that he was a mlungu, he still couldn't be trusted. No matter what Meena said.

But he did have a car.

I rubbed the soap against my arms until the skin was raw. I got out and dried my body with a cloth. Then I took buckets of bathwater and threw them out, watching the pools of dirty water stream down the street.

# Jack

"IT'S IMPORTANT TO LEARN HOW TO PARALLEL PARK," I SAID. "So do it again."

"Why?"

"That's the only way you park cars in Soweto, so you might as well get good at it."

"Don't you have anything better to do?"

"Yes, but I'm here. So too late for me," I said.

She tried again, this time getting a better angle, but still not good enough.

"Reverse. Again," I said.

"Aye, thula *wena*," she said, taking the car out again and checking the mirror.

"And what's that mean?"

"It's shut up. But more polite."

"What are you doing now?" I said.

"I'm driving away, what does it look like? Enough parking."

This was the third driving lesson. Each time I waited on the side of the highway that skirted the mounds of mining waste, I was convinced she wouldn't come. And it was strange that I felt cheated, disappointed in that moment.

But she did come. Always choosing to ignore any mention of why I was really there. And that was fine—for her I was a new experiment, a mlungu who waited for her by landfills, opened car doors for her.

It was a sixty-mile speed limit, Zanele was doing maybe seventy. So it was not surprising that we were stopped.

"Pull over," I said. "It'll be worse if you don't."

She didn't say anything. Like me, she was calculating the probabilities of each move. She pulled over, letting the car take its time to slow down.

Behind us, a traffic policeman walked up to the car. He stared at Zanele, at her hands on the steering wheel, her long thin fingers. I looked straight ahead.

"Baas," Zanele said. "The policeman wants to talk to you." Her accent had suddenly changed.

The policeman took off his sunglasses.

I turned to him. "Hello, officer. What's the problem?"

He chewed and then spat out his tobacco on the street.

"The problem is that I see this car speeding. And then I see a black woman driving with a white man. That's the problem."

The policeman leaned in as Zanele opened the door on him—too fast. It hit his face, hard, and he fell back against the curb. Zanele accelerated, the door hanging open. In the rear-view mirror, the policeman's body moved. Then he was a speck, gone.

WE CAME TO A DEAD END, A COLLECTION OF SKIPS WITH rubbish spilling out, dogs and little children playing.

"The policeman is going to have your number plate," Zanele said, taking the key out of the ignition and holding it out. "You'll need a story."

"Thanks for the advice," I said.

She smiled.

"You knocked him out."

"Yes." She dropped the keys onto the dashboard.

"Yes?"

"You shouldn't be surprised, mlungu. That is the kind of person I am."

I tugged at the collar of her black shirt and pulled her close. Her lips grazed mine and I was lost for a moment.

Then she pulled away. "We cannot see each other again," she said.

Which was what I was going to say. "Yes, obviously."

"And don't be angry, mlungu. It doesn't suit you," she said, stepping out of the car. "Remember. Your story."

RICKY PUSHED THE WHISKY BOTTLE INTO MY CHEST. "COME, Jacky, another one." He was acting drunker than he was. Oliver poked at the last lot of meat on the *braai*.

Megan, in her best black dress, was smoking a cigarette on the other side of the porch pillar.

Ricky rocked on his heels and stared at her bare back. "Don't know how you do it, Jack."

"Do what?"

"Get someone like that to stick around. Where have you been these last few days? Oliver thinks you're planning another *jol* for us."

"And what do you think?"

"You're messing around."

"You got that in one," I said.

Ricky sat back against the table and looked at me. "Tell me, Jacky."

"Sometimes you get bored, and you do stupid things," I said. "There's nothing to tell."

Megan leaned down and put her cigarette into the ashtray next to me. Then she took another one out of the pack. I ground her stub into the ashtray.

"More like you're telling me nothing."

"Try not to get into the kind of trouble I got into, Ricky. I wouldn't recommend it."

I left them on the porch, stepping on the dead crickets scattered on the tiles. Suddenly I thought of Zanele's shoulders, her collarbones against the red dress straps in the dim streetlight, the first time I'd seen her. And the way she held my shirt in her hands, so angry.


## Zanele

I WAS SITTING IN THE LONG YELLOW GRASS TELLING THE OTHER students about the protest, like Vusi asked. He called this "making student cells." All his talk of shadows, a secret army, and I was sitting out in the sun with Soweto's loudest grade twelves, arguing with them. Cars passed by on the highway. Some seemed to slow near us. Some were red. But it was not the mlungu's.

The students were from Orlando West, Jabavu, Naledi and Phefeni. Most of them I'd either seen in debates or hanging around the shebeen. Some of them were the kind who picked fights with other students, tsotsis or whoever they could find. And some were the ones who started fights and then stood back, watched. I needed the troublemakers.

"So you say all this. How you going to do it?" one of them asked. The others stuck their faces closer.

"We're going to have a meeting—"

"Meetings, meetings, meetings, *suka* wena, that's all you people say," Winston, from Naledi, said, getting up to leave. I put my hand on his shoulder, felt his muscles tighten. It would be easy for him to throw me off, like throwing off a fly. The other students watched. If Winston left, they'd leave too.

Slowly, Winston sat down again. But he was angry. I dropped my hand.

"This meeting, it's not like any of the others," I said. "It's the meeting before the strike. So you better believe it's happening."

"There was a strike in Phefeni last month," Winston said. "And nothing is better. So what do you expect now? Just because Zanele decides there's a protest, the Boers will say, 'Sorry, sorry, Zanele. We will change the baas law, just for you.'"

"At least we tried at Phefeni," a boy interrupted.

"So what?" a boy from Orlando West shouted. "You wrote some signs and walked around the school."

"We chased the principal out of school."

"Ja, looking at your principal, it's not a hard thing to do."

"This time everyone is coming," I said, shouting over them. "All the schools. Too many to ignore."

"Which ones?" Winston said.

I turned my arm over and showed him the signatures there, of the student representatives from all the different schools.

They ran their fingers over the names. There was Masi's, a bit bigger than the others. And Themba's. And Vusi's, which was small, almost invisible in black ink near my elbow.

"June 13th," I said.

"June 13th. *Amandla!*" someone shouted, and the boy from Phefeni raised his fist. It stuck out, black against the yellow grass. Then there were other fists up against the grass.

And then I went home and washed the names off my arm.

## Meena

"LAST TIME I CAME, YOU WERE NOT HERE," SAID JONAS. THE Mercedes waited at the curb, dirtier than usual, and no blond man in sight.

"I have school," I said, putting tuna cans up on our tinned-food shelf.

"School," said the man. "That is very good. You must keep studying."

"Yes," I said.

"What do you study?"

"What other students study."

"And what's that?"

"Maths. Physics. Biology. You don't have any children?"

"I did, *wena*, but that was a long time ago."

I finished stacking the cans and moved to the counter. Jonas sat on Papa's stool and looked absently at the ceiling. I rang up two packs of Lucky Strikes. The longer Jonas stayed, sat on the stool, talked to me about random things, the more I wanted him to leave. There was only so much talking you want to do with a policeman's driver who loves his baas.

"Your father, he plays too much of that Indian music," Jonas said. "You must tell him it's too much."

"Your baas, he's not here today?" I fidgeted with the packs, slid them across the counter. But Jonas didn't take them.

"He is here, in the township, working. You know, he does the difficult work. He has to find the troublemakers, the ones who cause all the problems, want to put bombs in the trains, eish, last month it was the power station." Jonas shook his head. "Eish, it's not good."

"They are angry at the government."

"Me, I was angry at the government. At white people," said Jonas. "But I didn't blow things up. I listened. I did my job. And my baas, he helped me." He coughed. Small tears escaped his lids, and streamed down his marked face.

I hesitated, then took the bottle I'd taken from Dr A.'s last week and passed it over. "This might help for the cough."

Jonas picked it up and tipped it so that the light caught the liquid. He smiled.

From the symptoms I'd described, Dr A. had guessed that it was miliary tuberculosis. A common strain among miners. Dr A. told me that if the symptoms where as bad as I was describing them, and the man was that far gone, he had little chance of living past the year.

Under the microscope, he said, miliary TB showed itself by small light and dark spots indented in the lungs. Some of the cuts would grow longer, deeper, over time. It was probably already happening.

I wondered about the family he'd not mentioned. The children that had been. And about his baas he never failed to praise. I wondered if they'd grieve for Jonas.

# Thabo

I REMEMBERED THE FIRST TIME I DID A BIG JOB FOR MY GANG. It was in a parking lot near Orlando West, where we dropped the *dagga* for Sammy to collect. This man I'd come for was stealing from us.

He was thin, light brown. Probably more coloured than black. His eyes never looked straight.

I strangled him, my hands on his throat, his back pressed against a car. At the last moment before he stopped breathing, I let go and walked away.

I don't know why I thought about it today, but it just came. Sizwe had told me to think of it as giving back a life. I let him live, that snake of a man. And then Sizwe spat on my new shoes, missing the floor. But I didn't say anything. You don't tell Sizwe he dirtied your shoes. Never.

WE SPENT THE MORNING CLEANING THE BAR, PREPARING THE line-up, and then I told the boys their route for the day, gave them the dagga. There was still a bandage on my hand from that Indian girl and her blunt knife.

Later in the morning, Zanele visited me. I knew she wanted something.

So I waited for her to stop looking at the floor.

"Something happened," she said.

"Ja, so what is it."

"In Houghton."

When she said Houghton, I knew there was something more to it.

"Number plates. On a car."

I looked at her. "Number plates, a car, Houghton. So?"

"The policeman was chasing us, we got away. Now the policeman has the licence plate number. Thabo, what can I do?"

I shook my head at Nkosi. He was putting the glass in the wrong place. And it had a big thumbprint on it. I took it down. "Do it properly," I said. "I want to see my face in it."

Zanele grabbed my shoulder. "You're not telling me what to do."

"Whose car are you talking about? Whose plates?"

I HAD TO HAVE A LONG CONVERSATION WITH MANKWE TO FIND out the mlungu's address. Finding out things from her these days was easier because her mind stayed with Professor. All her songs had become sad, and some of the regulars were starting to complain. But I didn't say anything. I left her alone.

Then, after seeing Mankwe, I had to steal some old man's pass into Houghton.

I took Nkosi with me into town. The bus took the bridge over the train tracks that connected downtown to where the mlungus lived. As the bus came onto the bridge, the five o'clock trains came in under it, their yellow-striped faces taking turns to stop at the station, long rust-coloured carriages going on and on till your eyes got tired of looking at them. People flooded from the third-class carriages, so many men in their ugly blue and green overalls.

To the tsotsi, the train is a blood vessel, you can say. The easiest place to take a wallet or a watch when you're running out of a rand, fifty cents. When a tsotsi gets more experienced, he prefers to go across the bridge on a fake or stolen pass, and steal from mlungus. It's easy to steal from mlungus. Above everything, they hate being touched by blacks. So you touch the mlungu on the chin, he becomes so angry, he doesn't notice you've taken his wallet. A few of you take him on all sides, take him down quickly. His watch, his wallet. Cufflinks.

I turned away from the window as the boy stared at the trains. You couldn't blame him, he'd spent more than half his life in Transkei, where you are lucky if you see something move faster than a goat. We crossed the bridge, came closer to Houghton.

After a while, Zanele understood that there was nothing she could do. Just wait, see, hope. A policeman hit by a black girl is not going to forget it. She wanted me to tell her it wasn't anything to worry about, but I didn't. Zanele didn't like people telling her lies. She blamed you later.

She told me not to be stupid, not to try anything. I didn't agree or disagree. Like I said, no lies with Zanele. But I'd decided from the time she mentioned the abo gata that I was going to have to do something.

And it wouldn't be such a hard job for me to make sure the mlungu didn't tell the police who she was. Even if the mlungu gave a different name for Zanele that would be enough. The police couldn't find a black without a passbook number and a name.

All the way to the mlungu's house, I was trying to figure out how the mlungu and Zanele ended up in his car together. I don't take so long to understand things, usually.

THE FORD MUSTANG WAS PARKED OUTSIDE THE GATE. NKOSI whistled when he saw it. When I came closer, I knew it was very old and had a light broken.

There was no guard in the guardhouse.

I waited by the curb and told Nkosi to walk up to the gate, see if he saw anybody inside. He came back, shook his head. I handed him a screwdriver.

"You use it on the car," I said, pointing. "There, on the side."

The boy just looked at me.

"When I tell you something, you do it, wena," I said, taking the screwdriver from him and making a nice clean line through the red paint.

Then I saw the mlungu walk down from his house. I stood

up. He was alone. This was good.

Nkosi, like an idiot, stood up too, ready to fight.

"Finish what you are doing, *mfana*." I pushed him back down. "You don't get up unless I say."

The mlungu struggled with the gate, opened it. He was taller than me. Now that he was close, I realized I had seen him before. At Pillay's.

He came right up to me and said, "What are you doing?" It's funny, how the English mlungu tries to pretend he's not scared. At least the Afrikaaner's honest. If he was going to hit you, no polite conversation first.

The mlungu moved toward the boy, but I went in front of him.

"I'm here for a message."

"Message?"

"Message for you."

"I see. What kind of message."

"You don't say anything to the policemen when they ask you about the girl. Nothing. Or you are finished." I pressed one finger into his neck. Then two, so that he could understand how it would feel if he told. And like the stupid mlungu he was, he tried to twist my arm away. Then he put his arm around my neck. Mistake. I threw him over my back and he hit the ground hard.

Then I punched him. His skin was soft, too soft, like you would expect from a mlungu who spent all his time inside. I tried to punch him again, but he moved aside and got to his feet. Then he hit me, harder than I expected.

He looked at me like he thought I was going to fall. I hit him. He tried to get up again, but I put a foot on his shoulder.

"You go back to your house, and make sure you say nothing to the police. Otherwise I will make sure they find you tomorrow on the railway tracks."

The mlungu stared at my bow tie. Blood ran down his face.

He smiled. "I know who you are. You're Zanele's thug."

I hit him hard this time, my knuckles crashing into his teeth. Then he caught my arm and held it, just waiting, staring at me with his pale, almost transparent mlungu eyes. Behind him, I saw someone run down from the house with a rifle. Probably his father.

I leaned down and pulled the mlungu's neck toward me. The father stopped. I kept my arm around the boy's neck.

"Thabo," said Nkosi.

"What?" I said.

"I'm done."

"Good," I said, seeing the long deep scratches in the paint. "Now run."

At least the boy could run when you told him to.

It made me sad that I couldn't kill the mlungu. I pushed him to the ground.

Then I ran. And the father started shooting.

## ELEVEN

# Zanele

I KEPT THINKING ABOUT WHAT JACK WOULD DO WHEN THE police questioned him. I told Thabo about it and his face told me it would be bad. And he didn't know that it wasn't my first time in the mlungu's car.

After we got away, Jack stopped the car. He tried to kiss me. I almost let him. He smelled of aftershave, peppermint. He wasn't used to being angry with someone and at the same time wanting them.

He was wishing I wasn't black. I knew that.

He was used to getting what he wanted, and this time he couldn't.

I didn't know what I liked about him. He surprised me. Maybe it was that he could be so quiet, the way he smiled suddenly for no reason. The way he never talked about his life. And the laughing light in his eyes.

THABO CAME BACK WITH HIS MOUTH BLOODY AND SWOLLEN. I wiped the blood off with a cold wet cloth.

"The mlungu won't say anything to the abo gata now," he said.

I knew why.

"He needed a lesson."

"I shouldn't have told you."

"Ja? Who else?"

The oil lamp flickered in and out. In the dim light, it was hard to see how bad Thabo's face was. I put a hand on his forehead. He held it there and smiled, a hole where one of his teeth had been knocked out.

I wondered if Jack could still walk.

I wiped off Thabo's face again, listened to him talk. I knew that if Jack came to see me again, I wouldn't turn him away. But he wouldn't. Not after this.

## Meena

ONE OF THE TSOTSI'S TEETH WAS GONE. TWO HAD GONE already, replaced by shiny metal. I think the tsotsi liked showing them off—his smile made sure you saw them every time. "Where's it gone? Someone stole it?" I said.

"Thula wena," he said. "When I say you be quiet, you be quiet."

Dr A. filled out the report. "Thabo, I am not going to clean you up every time you fight with the Ivies, The Hazel or whoever."

Thabo sneered. "Aye wena, Dr A., don't confuse me with the Ivies. All they do is dress in pretty clothes. This girl here can fight better than them."

"Okay. Educate me. Which gang was it, then?" Dr A. asked.

"This wasn't one of the boys here. No, I had to go up to Houghton this time. But it's okay, the mlungu is much worse than me."

"Was it Jack?" I said. "Jack Craven?"

"I don't know the name of every mlungu I moer." He spat.

"Bandage for tomorrow?" I said, holding it out.

"Take it, Thabo," said Dr A.

Thabo took the sachet holding the bandage, dropped it in the bin, and walked out.

Dr A. leaned down and took it from the bin. "There are

some people—you keep fixing them until it's too late."

I took off my gloves and threw them in the bin. I washed my face and hands.

WHEN I WALKED OUT OF THE CLINIC AT SIX O'CLOCK, A HAND went over my mouth, and I was pressed against the wall.

"How did you know about the mlungu," the tsotsi asked.

An old lady stared at us, then trotted out of sight.

"Just tell me," he said.

I nodded.

He took his hand off.

"When we were at the PAC meeting a few days ago," I said slowly. "We were caught by the police. And then this white guy came out of nowhere in his red car and lied to the police for us. Then we went into his car and drove away. Zanele didn't trust him but she knew him."

Which was the truth, but not all of it. I looked at the tsotsi, to see his reaction. But his expression didn't change.

"Then the next day, at the shop—" I continued.

"He came there when I was there," the tsotsi interrupted. "He's the one you told me to take the money from."

"I didn't tell you."

"You did. And you told him where Zanele was. Fok. You make a mess of everything."

"I didn't mean to," I said. "Please, I need to go home."

"So go. Who's stopping you?" he said, impatiently. The tsotsi rubbed his head, turned to walk in the direction of the bus rank.

"Wait," I said, and realized that I was running after him. Running after the tsotsi. I grabbed his arm. "There's more to the white guy story."

"What else?" he said, and stopped.

"Maybe we don't know the whole story."

"What are you saying?"

"Be careful," I said, and then dropped his arm. Then the tsotsi was gone.

## Jack

SUPERINTENDENT JOUBERT LOWERED HIMSELF ONTO OUR couch. The two policemen who came with him stood politely, one under each kudu head.

"Come a little closer, boy," Joubert said. "Let me have a look."

Obviously he was enjoying it.

"Sorry about calling you last minute, Johan," my mother said. "We didn't know what else to do."

"This one meant business," Joubert said. "Look, the way he hit you. One of those gangs. Probably was going for the house. Goodness knows what would have happened if he'd made it there. Did you hear about the family up in Sandton—"

"He was short, and he had a kid with him. And he didn't have a gun," I interrupted. Joubert enjoyed his morbid fancies, but I wasn't in the mood for hearing about a family being slaughtered in their homes by rogue blacks. My mother came in with another ice pack and patted my face with it.

"That's the problem, my boy. You underestimated him," Joubert said. "You must never underestimate that kind of black. You know what happened the other day? One of my traffic officers was assaulted by one of their women. They're savages, all of them."

My mother pressed a hand to her chest, her default gesture for expressing shock.

"Don't worry, we have the number plate. It's only a matter of time to track it down." His eyes moved from my mother to me. Lingered.

"Which kind of black is that?" I said.

"Hah?" asked Joubert.

"You said that I shouldn't underestimate some kind of black. Which type are you talking about?"

"Shhh," Mother said.

"We'll need a full report on this," Joubert said. "A full one. Hendrik, come here. Ask him all the questions."

"That's the full report," I said. "I saw some people near my car. It was a boy and some gangster. I'd never seen them before. They beat me up, scratched my car and then they left. That's it."

# Zanele

"Thabo asked me where Mama's Madam lived," Mankwe said, leaning up from her bed. "Why did he want to know where they live?"

"I don't know," I said, rinsing the dishes in the bucket.

"You don't know?"

"No," I said.

"Tell me, Zanele. Did you always lie to me like this, or am I just noticing it now?"

"I am not the only one who keeps secrets," I said. "You didn't tell me about Professor."

"You never asked. I was going to marry him, and you never noticed. Maybe it's not your fault you're selfish, Zanele," Mankwe said in a quiet voice. "Baba was like that too."

"Don't ever say that. Ever."

I dried the dishes and tied my hair up for school. I wanted to cry with her for the husband she had lost. I wanted to tell her that it was better she didn't know what was going on with me. But I didn't.

# Jack

IT TOOK ME A FEW DAYS. FINALLY I TOOK MY WRECKED CAR
back into Soweto, back to Zanele's shack with its yellowed tin
walls. She was wearing a blue and black school uniform and
had her hair tied back. I got out of the car. She stopped when
she saw me. She was wearing black sandals with rounded tops,
the kind small girls wear. And it was strange that she was here,
right in front of me.

"He really did beat you up," she said.

"Pity you weren't there to watch. Or were you?"

"He came to warn you. You shouldn't have fought back."

"I haven't come here for an argument. Or even a polite
conversation. Don't send him to my home again. Otherwise I
will tell the police exactly where to find you."

"I didn't send him there. It doesn't matter if you don't
believe me. Just remember the story you're going to tell the
police, your mother."

She looked tired. She tugged her hair out of its elastic. "Go
back in your car, and never come here again."

I said nothing.

She put a hand on my shoulder. "What do you want?"

There was the sound of hooting cars and yelling.

"I don't know," I said.

She leaned in, her eyes resting on my face.

Then she kissed me.

Her hand dropped from my shoulder and she stepped back.
"Now, go."

But I stayed, took her face in my hands.

AFTERNOONS, WE WOULD DRIVE OUT TO THE VELD, OR SIT IN
the car in some side street.

Once, I went to her home. He mother was working late.
From my car, I watched her sister leave for the shebeen.

At her door, she stared at me like I was a stranger. Like she'd forgotten that, just a few days before, we'd kissed in my car, and in the tall grass. She stepped aside to let me in. I stood, stooped under the low ceiling. It smelled of cooked oats and mud. On one side of the room, a large metal bathtub was stacked on bricks.

She waited by the door.

"Why don't you want me to come in?"

"I didn't say that."

"You didn't need to."

She walked through a thin plastic curtain separating the room and came out with a sequined dress coiled up in a ball. The shebeen dress. "I don't think we should be meeting in each other's houses."

"You came to mine," I said, regretting it as soon as I said it. "I didn't mean it like that."

"I don't know, Jack. Maybe you did." Her voice was flat, unfamiliar.

She put on lipstick, facing a shard of mirror stuck to the wall.

As I left she said, "Don't come here again."


## Zanele

I LIKED IT THAT JACK DIDN'T TELL STORIES ABOUT HIS childhood, his parents, what he ate for breakfast. He didn't talk about the weather, or rugby, and he didn't seem to read the newspapers.

"So then what do you talk about?" I asked him once.

"Mostly different combinations of nothing," he said, putting an arm over his face.

"That's not true."

"Trust me, it is," he said, half smiling.

"There has to be something you want to talk about. What are you going to study at university?"

"Maths," he said, and rolled over, closing his eyes.

"Why?"

He groaned, lifted his head off my lap. "I have to answer this, hmm?"

I sat up, brushing the grass off my skirt. He traced my cheek with his fingers and kissed my neck, the line of my jaw, then my lips.

ANOTHER TIME HE TOLD ME ABOUT IMAGINARY NUMBERS. They weren't real but if you tinkered with them, you could get real answers.

"They're used to calculate electrical currents," Jack said. "You have a real answer that can be used to measure the right amount of electricity needed to power the city."

I almost told him about the power station then.

"You're not interested in this," he said. "So why are you letting me talk about it?"

"You don't know that. So when do you start at Wits? Next year?"

He hesitated. "Soon."

"Why are you here with me?" I said. "You have your life, I have mine. It's better that way."

"I told you before," he said patiently. "I like you. It's not really more complicated than that."

"You like me because you're not allowed to."

"Then that's true for you too."

I didn't answer.

"Of course, of course you don't give me an answer," he said, turning away from me. Not angry. Jack never got angry.

I knew that if I asked him to stay longer, miss the dinner with his friends, he would. So I did, and said I didn't feel like talking. He just sat next to me, his hand carelessly over my knees. I don't know how long we just sat there.

He surprised me. How he didn't try to understand everything I did, or tell me what to do.


# Jack

"ONE CONDITION," SHE SAID, INTERRUPTING ME. I WAS JOKING about the pamphlets she'd thrown around at those schools.

"Ja, what?"

"Don't ask about that."

"What does that mean?"

"It means, don't ask me where I go, what I do. Don't expect an answer."

I thought about Oxford. But since she had her secrets, there was no need to mention it. "That's not hard," I said. "You seem to think that I'm going to be chasing you around everywhere, wanting to know everything you do."

"But you chase me all around Soweto."

"I'm not doing any chasing at the moment," I said.

We were on a hill that looked over the train tracks, and it was six o'clock. Her skin was soft, warm, as if she were running a fever. Her eyes followed the crowd pouring out of the trains onto the platform.

"Why do you think they do it?" she asked me.

"What?"

I tried to see what she saw in the swarm of black people— maids, hotel bell boys who are not boys but men, carrying their uniforms in carefully sealed plastic bags.

"I'm not going to answer that question."

"Why?"

"It's one of your trick questions. You want to trap me into

some stupid answer, and then keep reminding me of what a terrible mlungu I am."

"You can't even say the word correctly. It's mlungu."

"Okay."

"Anyway, don't try and get away from the question like you always do. Just be serious for a moment. Look at them. Why do they do that day after day?"

She propped herself on her elbows and looked at me, pieces of yellow grass in her hair. And I was jealous, painfully jealous of the gangster, all the other shebeen boys—how they were part of her life, how they could see her here, like this, whenever they wanted. But I turned to look at the train instead, at the people. I thought of Lillian, when she came in the morning to clear away breakfast. Light scars on the side of her face.

"They do it to survive. Okay, go ahead, tell me I'm wrong."

But she didn't say anything.

"Ah, so that means I'm right."

"Something might happen soon to change all this," she said.

"How specific of you."

She had made a fist, the thumb coming up and over the other fingers. "Amandla."

"I've told you, speaking to me in Zulu or Xhosa repeatedly is not going to make me understand it better."

"It means power."

"I'll keep that in mind."

"You should." Her eyes returned to the figures on the platform.

## Zanele

HE'D SAID TO ME ONCE: "I'M NOT LIKE THIS WITH OTHER people, you know. I tell you what I'm thinking, mostly."

"Thank you for that gift. If only I could sell it, or trade it for something useful, like coal or meat."

"Hey—I offered you money before, remember, the first time. And you didn't want it. So now you've just got this. Me."

Like he would ever belong to anybody.

"Looks like I made the wrong choice."

"Ja, looks like you did."

I remember the dust floating in his car. The mlungu knew that I knew that he was trying to make me like him more, say or promise something that I couldn't. I remember the smell of his newly washed shirt. An expensive brand of washing powder only for mlungus.

# TWELVE

## Jack

AT DINNER, THE CUTLERY FELT COLD AND HEAVY IN MY HANDS. These days, I had less and less to say to my parents. My father, with no Van Roonens present, made no effort to make conversation. So it was left to my mother to talk us through the meal, and she talked and talked. My eyes wandered from her face to the windows, to the over-tended garden. I saw everything in a new unpleasant light that made it difficult to carry on as I had.

In a few months, it would be time to leave for England anyway.

"SO WHAT DO YOU THINK?" MEGAN SHIFTED IN FRONT OF THE mirror, pressing the dress against her body.

The shop attendant chimed in. "Looks very classy on you, the white really goes with your hair."

"You're putting a lot of thought into this," I said.

"It's your farewell. As Ricky says, we've got to go all out." Megan carried it over to the till.

I pulled out my wallet.

She put her hand over mine. "Don't be silly."

"Don't worry about it." I drew my hand away, handed the shop attendant the money and slid the dress across the counter. The small beads were cold and hard. Soon my mother would tell Lillian to lay out white streamers through the trees. Then dancing on the lawn till one or two.

The shop attendant packed the dress in tissue paper.

We walked to the car in silence. The Mustang looked

particularly broken and dusty in the pale afternoon light. I opened the door for Megan, closed it shut.

"You're like your father."

"What?"

"You insist on acting like some kind of English gentleman, paying for everything and opening doors for me. But you couldn't care less about me."

"Thanks for that," I said. "Finally figured out my parents' relationship."

"I'm not blaming you for dropping me, Jack, I'm just making an observation."

"Dropping you?"

"Barely even noticed. Thought so."

I didn't reply.

As WE STOPPED OUTSIDE HER HOUSE, SHE LEANED OVER, HER hair grazing my face. I moved away before she could kiss me.

"See," she said.

"I'm as surprised as you are," I said. And I was.

"I'm not surprised."

She stepped out of the car and walked up her driveway, the shopping bag tight in her hands.

I RETURNED HOME WITH A PACKAGE IN WHITE PAPER. A SATIN dress, no beads. I knew Zanele would dislike the dress, dislike that I'd bought it for her. But this was very little about Zanele's feelings, more to soothe mine. Sometimes we do things to make ourselves feel like we can do whatever we want, when we can't.

# Thabo

YOU ONLY HAVE TO SEE IT ONCE, AND YOU DON'T NEED TO SEE the whole thing to know. Mustangs are very rare, especially in this part of the city. And this one was a red scratched one. Very rare. Zanele stepped out of it, looking left, right. Even though she looked, she didn't see me and Sizwe on the other side of the closed-off street.

And the only reason I didn't go right then to the mlungu's car was because Sizwe was there. If I did anything, even made a face, Sizwe would turn around and see what I had seen.

Now I walked slowly to the bus rank. I waited for the seven pm and then the eight. At nine she came, still in her uniform.

"Zanele," I called out.

She looked up but didn't smile when she saw me. This was something I had not noticed before, but maybe it was always that way. Maybe I just lied and lied to myself. She walked toward me, and we walked together to her shack.

I wanted to hurt her. But I didn't.

"So why the mlungu?"

"What?"

"Don't pretend," I said. "I know. I saw you with the mlungu. In his car."

Zanele didn't even look ashamed. She didn't try to lie, say it was someone else. No.

All she said was, "Oh."

Then she turned away to go inside. I took her hand, held her back. "Why? Why the mlungu!"

She tried to pull away. "Thabo, I don't know."

"You think the mlungu is better than us."

Zanele pushed me and we fell. Her nails dug into my shoulders. Zanele held my shoulders down, her hair falling on my face. Then she got up, off of me.

I got up slowly. "All this time, Zee, I've taken your kak. But this time, this time I hate you."

"I know," she said. It looked like she was going to cry. Something I hadn't seen in a long time. But I wasn't sure if she was crying for me or the mlungu.

I walked away.

## Zanele

ONE BY ONE, STUDENTS FROM EACH SCHOOL STOOD UP TO SAY whether they would join us. They held up their right hands in fists. Some of them looked at me.

Soon there would be a thick snake of students all the way from Morris Isaacson to Orlando Stadium.

Masi came to the front in a green shirt, waving. And the crowd became quiet. He held his hands out. "We have waited a long time for them to listen to us. But they will not listen to us. So we will march. We will not fight them. We will just march."

Students muttered.

"But if they try to fight us, we will defend ourselves."

The crowd surged forward, excited and loud. Masi held them back with his hands. "Are we ready for June 16?" he shouted. "Are we ready?"

A cheer went up. Everyone stamped and the floor shook.

Vusi joined me in the corner of the room and held out a pack of cigarettes and a lighter.

"Congratulations," he said.

I waved his cigarettes away. "For what?"

"For this," he said. "In the history books, they will write about Masi, about the SASM members. But you did it too."

"It doesn't matter," I said. "Nothing's happened yet. Stop dreaming about history books."

Vusi exhaled, smoke rose slowly to the dirty ceiling. People were leaving in small groups.

Masi put his hat on and nodded to us.

"We are going to change all their lives. Do you believe me?" Vusi said, staring at Masi, the students clustered around him.

"Yes," I said. "Because, if I don't, there's nothing left to fight for."

I turned the light off in the hall and we left, walking in different directions. A police car slid next to the sidewalk, slowing down but not stopping. I kept my head down and didn't change my pace.

My home was quiet and empty. I tried to sleep, thinking about how I'd lost Thabo for good.

## Meena

ZANELE CAME IN TO BUY RED LIPSTICK.

"How's what's his name, Jack, doing?" I said, looking down at the cold black tube as it rolled across the counter to me.

"I don't know," she said, and let the words hang there, clarifying nothing.

I tallied up the lipstick purchase and put the tube in a bag. I hadn't expected Zanele to be so serious about the white boy. So serious that she wouldn't tell me.

"It was a question," I said. "That's all."

"I know. It doesn't matter."

But it did.

"It's finally happening," she said.

"What?"

Zanele leaned forward across the counter as three of my father's friends entered the store. "Sixteen June. Keep an eye out."

"For what?"

Zanele flashed my father's friends a large fake smile, then left.

## Zanele

I WOKE UP THE NEXT MORNING TO SEE MAMA STANDING AT our window, tying up her braids. They were thick, good for tying in one piece. As she stood against the morning light, working with her hair, she smiled. She probably didn't even notice. But then the cap was over her hair, and when she turned from the window she wasn't smiling anymore.

"Are you ready?" she said. "Zanele, I am talking to you."

"Mama, I can't go with you," I said.

"Tell me, Zanele, why can't you come and help me? Why is it so difficult? Tell me."

THERE WERE WHITE STREAMERS THROUGH THE TREE IN THE old playground. Piano music drifted from the house. Then the breathy voice of some American woman, who kept telling Jack to hit the road and never come back.

This time we walked in through the front door. I went into the kitchen and did what Mama told me to do. My hands sunk into sugary dough again and again. Upstairs, maybe Jack was putting on a tie and pulling at the knot so that it was straight under his throat.

"Mrs Craven? Jacky boy?" A boy came through the door. He carried a bottle of wine and looked like he had been squeezed into his suit. He stared at me but didn't recognize me from that time he had come to the shebeen with Jack. He was wearing the same ugly light blue leather jacket then, too. He backed out of the kitchen, joining the others on the landing.

We pushed the pastry in the muffin pans and put the jam inside them. Then we covered it over with more pastry. Before we put the tray in the oven, Mama made small patterns on the top.

I wish I had never seen Jack's friends. I wish I had never seen this house. What was Mankwe's word for me? Careless. Jack and I had been careless, but he could afford to be.

## Jack

I FIRST SAW HER STANDING BEHIND THE PIANO AS MY FATHER was toasting me. His hair was thinning in the front, and as he stood with his champagne flute held against the light, that part of his scarred forehead glowed. I had assumed she wouldn't be coming. So I hadn't even thought to check with my mother. She was looking at my father in a cold irritated way. That was when my father said, "Because we all know that Jack will be happy to leave us in this backwater, while he conquers the world. Starting with England."

"I'M GLAD YOU'RE HERE," I SAID, PUTTING MY HANDS ON HER shoulders as she tacked up pictures in her mother's room in the maid's quarters. They were pictures of her and her sister, and then some older women. The edges of some of the photographs were chopped off. In some pictures, a disembodied man's hand or a shoulder in a shirt remained. Some of the pictures had been shot from odd angles, so it was hard to see faces.

She turned. I looked for any sign of how she had taken the news about Oxford. It was impossible to tell.

She turned back and kept pasting the pictures.

"You're not going to say anything?" I said.

"No. I need you to go."

"Why?"

"Jack, you are in the maid's quarters," she said.

I turned away from the wall and faced her. Her eyes met mine and then switched back to the photographs.

Even though she wasn't looking at me, I could tell she was angry, in her cool quiet way.

The maid's cap highlighted the sharpness of her features, the set of her mouth, the inherent irony of her being a servant to anyone.

"Why these pictures on the wall?"

"Don't think I'm coming back here. Might as well do it now."

"What does that mean?"

"You need to go back to the party in case they're looking for you."

"This is the first time you've heard of England, and you're saying nothing."

She put the photographs down. "Jack—maybe you want this to be your moment of truth, but I have other things to worry about. This is not the first time I've heard of England, of mlungus going to England. Just go."

"We'll talk later, okay?"


"COME, HONEY. DANCE WITH YOUR MOTHER."

As I took her out on the lawn, her body felt cold and fragile. She'd had too much sherry, and it was early.

My father watched us from inside the living room.

Megan watched us too, our slow half dance on the grass. She clapped slowly as the music drifted in and out.

Lillian came out with a tray of champagne glasses. She looked up, watching my mother and me, and started walking over with the last glass on the tray. And then my mother stumbled, knocking over the tray. The champagne spilled down the back of her dress.

"Watch what you're doing." My mother's voice was loud and shrill, cutting through the cold air.

"Madam, I'm sorry." Lillian held out the napkin, my mother ignored it.

"Use just a bit of your brain, Lillian." My mother held the back of her dress away from her skin. "Really, if it's not too much to ask. Now go, take yourself and this glass away from here."

Lillian walked away, slow and deliberate.

"I'm so glad, Jack, that you're going to England. So proud of you." My mother turned back around and took hold of me again. Smelling even more of alcohol.

"I know."

"All I've ever cared about is your happiness. You know that."

"Yes."

She rested on my shoulder and closed her eyes. I saw the light on in the maid's quarters, a single figure sat there, watching.

And then the Jouberts arrived.

My mother left me to greet them. I followed, slowly.

"Can you believe he's off so soon?" my mother said, taking Joubert's arm. "It's already mid-June."

"Nice to see you, Anna, always nice to see you." But Joubert was looking at me. "Jack," he said.

"Yes?"

"Your face looks better."

"Thanks."

"We are going to talk about that," he said. He took hold of my shoulders and walked me away from the garden. My father had left the living room, didn't seem to be in the house.

Joubert walked me to my father's study and sat down in my father's chair.

"Sorry, Mr Joubert. Are you looking for my dad? Can I get you a drink?"

"No, no, nothing. You can sit down, Jack, my boy. Because I know." Joubert leaned back, smiling in a way that shrank his eyes into slits. "I know," he said again.

I sat, waited.

"The last time I came here, I remember mentioning the attack to you."

"What attack?"

"Don't act stupid with me, boy. The traffic policeman . . ." Joubert said, enjoying himself. "I told you we had the number for the licence plate on that car. So we tracked it down, and we found who the car belonged to."

"And who was that?"

He leaned forward. "You."

He waited for me to say something, so I said nothing.

"I knew it was you."

"Okay."

"How does a black girl get into a white man's car and then attack a policeman? Why would she be there, in this white boy's car?"

"Why don't you tell me?"

Joubert's face turned red. He stood up and leaned over me. "You broke the Immorality Act." His spit landed on my shirt and my face. "And that tsotsi was blackmailing you. He had come for the money, but you didn't have enough, so he beat you up."

"Very good."

"Who is the tsotsi's girl?" he asked me.

"None of your business." And there it was, my biggest slip up. I'd spoken too soon, too loudly, said the exact thing I shouldn't have said.

If only I'd gone along with him, said I'd picked her up somewhere and had no idea who she was. More disgusting to Joubert, but much better.

Joubert raised his eyebrows. "Interesting. I'm going to ask

you one more time. Because if you don't tell me, I will make sure this becomes public. If you break the law, you won't be able to go to your fancy school. Your family shamed."

"Come on, Mr Joubert. The police don't care about that kind of stuff like they used to."

"When there is an assault on a police officer, we care. Who is this black?"

I got up and buttoned my jacket. "Mr Joubert, if I tell you her name, what do I get in return? Your silence?"

Joubert said nothing.

"I thought not. So you see, there's really no point in me telling you who she is. I wouldn't be getting anything for it. You should really rethink the way you handle your interrogations."

"I will find her anyway," Joubert said.

"Good luck with that. I hear there are a number of women fitting her description all across Alexandria and Soweto."

## Zanele

THERE WERE FOUR GLASS CABINETS AGAINST THE WALL IN Jack's room. They were full of trophies and pictures of him with old mlungus putting medals around his neck.

Then there was a picture of Jack as a child, with his father. His father wore an army uniform and was leaning down, holding his rifle and his son. Jack's eyes were drawn away from the camera.

I went to Jack's desk. Sheets and sheets of tables with numbers, plotted lines, the same equation with small differences. I opened his drawers. There was very little in the first one, just a few paper clips, an extra wallet and a pocketknife. It was like him to have a few things in his drawers that could belong to anybody. In the trophy cabinet, behind

the trophies, some envelopes addressed to Jack Craven from
Oxford, England. I opened the envelope and flipped through
the pages of the brochure.

## Jack

WHEN JOUBERT AND I WALKED OUT OF THE STUDY, ALMOST
everybody was dancing. Zanele came out with the drinks.
Four flutes, amber yellow in the last of the sunlight. Joubert
and I parted and I started toward Megan, who was dancing
with Ricky. But there was Zanele, with Joubert right next to
me, and she about to speak to me. Not now.

"Not me. Offer that gentleman some," I said, waving my
hand in Joubert's direction. Then I walked away.

Megan's dress was soft against my hands. I leaned my head
against hers, but she tipped her head back. Joubert stood
holding his drink, watching me.

## THIRTEEN

### Zanele

I WENT OUT WITH THE DRINKS, OFFERING THEM TO JACK, THE Afrikaaner, Jack's father. Jack waved me off, without looking at me. I went back inside, finished cleaning the kitchen floor, the living room and the dishes. Mama was still doing the glasses.

· "Mama," I said. "I'm going back." I put my head against her strong broad back and my arms around her. I was letting her stay here, alone.

"Careful with the buses," she said, putting her hand briefly over mine.

### Jack

"SO ARE YOU GOING TO TELL ME?" MEGAN ASKED.

"Tell you what?"

"What was going on with Oliver's dad? And what's been going on with you these last few weeks? That's why I'm letting you dance with me."

Ricky was staring at Megan and me. He now had an arm around one of the girls who had gone to Rodean with Megan, a girl from Wits with a boyish haircut. As I watched, she shook him off.

"It's a good sign when a girl who's about to dump you still asks questions."

"You want it to end this way?"

"Worked so hard to get you to go out with me—"

"Very hard."

"Now this."

"Hmm."

I watched Joubert dancing with my mother. Then the light went off in the kitchen, and there was only Lillian's silhouette at the window in the maid's quarters.

"I'm sorry. I have to go now," I said.

"You do."

I walked past the slide and swings, to the porch. Trays of fruit had been left out, the outer skins of apricots and nectarines bruised by the afternoon cold.

I DROVE TO THE RANK, HONKED WHEN I SAW HER. I ROLLED DOWN the window.

"The police know," I said. "The Afrikaaner at the party is a colonel. Colonel Joubert."

"Then we shouldn't be seen together." She continued walking.

"He's dancing right now, busy. Get in. We'll make a plan."

She smiled strangely, got in the car. I pulled out and started driving her home.

"He doesn't know it's you," I said. "That's why I was like that with the drinks. And my mother was drunk."

"Please. Let us not talk about that."

"Look—"

"This Oxford University. You're going."

"You said—"

"I looked at all your notes. Your application. Don't let anyone stop you from doing what you want. If Joubert is threatening you, give him what he wants so that you can do what you want. That's what I would do."

"You're not serious." I braked a few streets away from her shack.

"How often, Jack, do I joke?"

"And what will you do then?" I said.

She put her head against my shoulder, and laughed.

"Why do you say things like that?" I said.

"I'm being honest."

She kissed my cheek. Then she got out of the car.

"I'll see you tomorrow," I said.

She turned and started walking toward her shack. Her back straight in her cheap cotton uniform. I imagined her bare back in the red shebeen dress.


## Zanele

I WALKED AWAY WITHOUT TURNING AROUND IN CASE HE WAS waiting for me to go back to him. He was patient.

In the end, he was a mlungu. They came and they went. So what did I expect?

But Jack wasn't afraid of apologizing—oh no, he would apologize all day long if that got him what he wanted.

I was cold. I had left my shawl and Mama behind. That was a mistake. I should have waited for Mama even though she hadn't asked me to. Instead of going home, I walked to the Orlando Power Station. The night was black—few streetlights here in Soweto, even now, after the government promised us electricity. And here and there, the calls of children, women and men from the shebeen. Somewhere out there, Masi and the rest were bent over, planning.

No lights and no street names, but I knew where I was going. I knew from years of walking with my hand in Baba's, in Mama's, in Mankwe's.

I walked. I saw a few men with their umqombothi, but they didn't see me. I thought of Professor. The new grass over his grave. Mankwe's wedding ring in tissue paper. I was standing at the edge of the township now, on the hill between the power station and the shacks. The station was still there, untouched. Phelele was gone. Billy was gone in his own way. And Masi and the rest of us were left behind.

The sky turned grey. The power stations were still, fat black shapes against the morning light. It would be a peaceful protest, and then a speech at the stadium. The government would just ignore it. I told myself all these things, but standing, looking down over Soweto, I felt like I was looking at the township for the last time.

I took the maid's cap off my head and threw it. It floated in the air for a few seconds then dropped onto a mound of mining waste. Wind blew the dust into my face. It was sharp and bitter in my mouth.

I walked back. Morning was coming, and it seemed as if I'd waited for this a long, long time—longer even than I'd been alive. I saw smoke rise from the shacks. Far off, the windows in the city glinted. The barking of dogs.

THE CHILDREN SLAPPED PAINT ON THE CARDBOARD SO THAT IT spattered on the ground, rose in small sprays in the air. The paint smelled of plastic and cut through the cold morning. I picked up a sawed-off piece of a door that said AWAY WITH BANTU EDUCATION, and carried it outside. The younger children followed me toward assembly, laughing and joking. I looked at the hundreds of them across the playground—a wave of bobbing heads. Like before a birthday party. But no cake.

No sign of the principal, the teachers. At least at our school they knew not to come. Good.

At the front, right before the gate that led out of the school, was Masi.

I felt the crowd pressing closer to him. Maybe they did because of his handsome face, his jokes, the way he made you

feel that you, alone, were important. I walked toward him—
he held his hands, palms out, trying to stop us.

I wondered why I'd never wanted him, wanted Jack instead.
A mlungu with a plane ticket to England—rolling green hills,
the land of mlungus.

Masi started singing. *Masibulele ku Jesu, ngokuba wasifela.*
It was the song we always had to sing for assembly, about
praising Jesus because he died for us. I started singing with
him. And then others did too—the song felt different now,
charged with something. Masi had found something in it that
we hadn't seen before.

Then Masi said: "One more song, just one." People laughed,
yelled. They waved placards over their thin arms, hitting each
other.

And then he started singing *Nkosi S'ikelele.*

Vusi came next to me, smiled. "Good choice," he said.
He put his fist on his chest, I did the same. In front of us,
Masi raised his fist. The crowd followed, with their fists and
then their placards, yelling "Amandla." Quietly, the teachers
had joined us. Mr Mamphile had a smile on his face and the
principal clapped slowly.

Then Masi told us to follow him.

We went out of the gate and onto the road. The street was
empty, waiting for us. And it was a little bit like the beginning
of a party, with the kids streaming out of the gate, the sound of
their voices loud and clear in the crisp morning air.

When we crowded into Thesele High School, we knew
they were not ready for us. Some of the teachers there stood
outside, looking terrified, some angry. Vusi grabbed my arm as
students pushed past us.

"We can't let them get a message out to the superintendent—
you understand?"

"You get the tires." I opened my bag, saw the tip of the

screwdriver glinting in it, and handed it to Vusi. Then I pushed past people and went around the back of the school, past the outdoor toilet, to the principal's office. The window looked onto a bare desk and the only telephone in the building. I had never broken a window before with my hand, but it shattered easily against my knuckles. I didn't hear the sound it made.

I climbed through the window, my school shoes scuffing against the bricks. I fell in on my back. I rolled over and got up. I shuffled through the desk. All the stationery had been laid out carefully in the drawer. I took out the scissors, found the black wire that connected the phone to the socket. Then I cut it.

I put the scissors back on the desk as the door opened and the principal came in. He picked up the receiver, started dialing. I rose slowly from behind the desk, holding out the cut wires.

"Sorry," I said. "Operator not available. The march won't be called off by a phone call to your mlungu superintendent."

As he reached out, his bulky body stretching over the desk, I climbed back out of the window into the crowd.

OUR STEPS MADE SHARP CRACKING SOUNDS AGAINST THE gravel of the road. People stopped on the street to stare at us. Cars stopped because the street was blocked now. We tapped their windows, told them to take another route. Some of them waved, shouted with us. Vusi was silent next to me. He was worried. Any moment the police could come.

When we crossed Mofolo Park, we saw the students from Naledi School, with Winston and Tina in front, her curls bouncing as she ran, children hanging on to her hands, her legs, everywhere. The students from Naledi didn't slow down as they came. We didn't either. When they ran into us, we hit and scraped each other until we swelled over the whole street right up to the doorsteps.

The noise and anger of the students was thick. They followed us, we carried them. Masi, Vusi and I.

"Do you feel it?" Vusi asked me.

I did.

# Thabo

"THABO, LOOK."

The Chevrolet Impala was old, but the man who owned it kept it nice. I had been eyeing it for some time, since before I became a tsotsi.

We were in a side street in Orlando West, the boys and I. I was teaching them how to steal cars, and this was an easy one. But Thulani, the smaller boy, was always distracted. I'd picked an easy target in case he made mistakes.

"Nkosi, hurry, smash the window," I told the older one.

The boy got off the roof of the car and found a stone. He tapped the window with it.

"Eish, Nkosi," I said. "That is not how you break a window."

That was when I saw what Thulani had been staring at: school blazers, maybe three hundred, headed this way. I got up on the car roof, getting my sleeves dirty.

Nkosi finally broke the glass and slipped inside. Thulani got in too. The students were waving signs, and more and more people were joining them, random street boys. I swore under my breath and slipped off the car roof. I pushed the boy out of the car seat and took the screwdriver from him, popping the ignition. It was too late. The old man had come out of his shop. He started shouting, waving his stick around.

I pushed the accelerator, and luckily the engine started. The old man ran after us, calling me dog, tsotsi, whatever he could think of. But he was left behind.

In the back seat, the boys cheered. I turned the radio on and the boys sang over it, loud. "Thula wena," I told them. I switched it off. "No need to celebrate. I was the one who stole the car. Now pay attention. We're going to drive into a riot."

They kept quiet as I drove the car toward the swarm of people. I stuck my head out of the broken window, and I waited for the crowd to reach us. But then I realized they would never reach us, because across the bridge, in six white vans, the abo gata were coming. I accelerated, knowing that I would be too late.

"Sisi Zanele is in there?" Thulani asked as we waited for a light to turn green.

The silence hung, Nkosi slapped him. "He will moer you if you say her . . ."

I said nothing and cut past the red light.

# Zanele

WHEN WE CAME TO THE BRIDGE, WE STARTED TRIPPING OVER each other. The placards ahead of me stopped, even though this was not a stop that we had planned, even though there didn't seem to be any cars blocking our way.

A hiss went through the crowd, which became a word that travelled down to me. Police. I lost Vusi as he ran ahead to find out if it was true. I didn't see him again.

Up ahead, Masi climbed up on the back of a truck. "We are not going to fight them," he said. "Just be calm."

Police.

Minutes passed and they didn't come. We started pushing each other, trying to go forward. Winston, the boy from Naledi, shouted, "Where's your police, eh, Masi?" A laugh went through the crowd.

Then we heard the sirens, the sound of rubber scraping road—three vans and four police cars. They formed into a line. The policemen got out, in khaki, with their dogs. The dogs, like their handlers, formed still shadows in the afternoon light.

It was their thick bodies, their dogs and their cars between Orlando Stadium and us. I elbowed students to get to the front, crushing placards under my feet. We came closer and closer to them.

"Stand back!" a policeman shouted through a loudspeaker. He was middle aged, with thick lines under his eyes and near his mouth. He tried it again in Zulu. "*Kahle!*" Then added that he was "serious."

I laughed at his attempt at Zulu. Some of the kids behind me started laughing too. The dogs strained on their leashes. Still, we came closer. The line of policemen looked like it was going to break.

A policeman with a child's face and a thin red beard stood opposite me, his fingers adjusting and re-adjusting on his gun. In a few seconds, I would be at his throat.

Then one of them threw something into the crowd, tossing it high above my head. Tear gas. Still we came at them.

A dog came loose from a leash and charged at us. Someone took a rock and threw it at the dog. And then others did too.

That's when the policeman with the red beard decided to shoot.

Someone shouted, and then we were all shouting. We found stones near our feet and threw them. More shots—we scattered, far and wide into side streets, slamming into shop fronts.

As I ran, I found small hands, and so I dragged them with me into an opening between two shops. I pressed their heads into the ground as more shots rang out. Students kept throwing stones. "Stop throwing," I screamed. "Stop throwing." My voice was gone, broken. A boy fell in front of me. Someone picked him up. Still the shots came. The boy was picked up by his friend. His blood fell onto the ground. A girl ran next to him, crying.

The children watched me with their large eyes.

I had not expected them to shoot us. I did not.

The violence took me back to the first days of drawing up plans with Billy, plans to bomb the tower. Back through all that had happened up to this moment.

I gripped the children's small bodies closer to me. The smoke, sweat, and the acrid taste of tear gas in my throat.

FOURTEEN

## Meena

"Stop the car," I said. "Here."

Prinesh, boasting about how he would soon get his own car, turned to look at me. "You're feeling sick?"

"No. Let me out here."

"What about school?" Krishni said.

"Make up an excuse for me." I gave her a fake smile, like Zanele, shut the car door and hurried toward the rank.

I folded my body into a seat and waited for the bus to fill up. A woman squeezed in next to me, something haggard, crazy in her face.

Halfway to Soweto, she said, "They're shooting our babies." Her mouth kept opening and closing after that, and no sound came out.

## Zanele

I heard the police drive away before I stood up.

"Stay close and be quiet," I told the children. We ran for cover behind a line of shops along the narrow street. It was strangely quiet, but I heard something scrape against the rubbish bins behind me. Someone was following us.

"Stop," I hissed. I looked behind the children, for a gun, a policeman, or a dog. Then someone turned me against the wall and held a knife at my throat. The children stopped and picked up stones.

"Don't," I shouted.

"Wise." I recognized the voice. He turned me around. It was Winston from Naledi, with blood on his face, his arm limp, under his shirt. "You brought the police here, with their dogs and the guns, sisi Zanele? This was part of your plan?"

"What? No."

"Someone warned the abo gata. How come they came so quick?"

"I don't know. Let me go."

He dropped me. I fell to the ground holding my throat.

"How do I know you didn't call them?"

"You can't know," Winston said. He stared at the children. "So what's your plan?"

"We need to get them home."

"With bullets in their bodies?" he asked. "Come on." He leaned down. My uniform grazed his bloodied clothes.

I didn't ask him where his friend Tina was.

"Regina Mundi," I said. "They won't shoot us in a church."

Winston cocked his head. "Maybe," he said, gesturing me to follow.

So I did. Behind me the children followed.

# FIFTEEN

## Meena

BOTTLES WERE BEING THROWN THROUGH THE CLINIC windows by children in school uniforms and boys in cheap suits. Tsotsis, but the fake kind. Some children were trying to stop them. They held hands, and their bodies circled around the clinic. I smelled smoke. Something was on fire.

Behind me, the crazed woman held onto my wrist and stared at the clinic. Zanele had told me something had been planned for today. And it had gone wrong.

I went to the back of the clinic, trying to find the source of the smoke. The crazy woman was still holding on to me.

I rounded the corner and hot flecks of oil and dirt hit my face and arms. I screamed. The woman next to me said nothing.

A fire at the back door was spreading fast. And a tall boy in a tattered shirt, maybe fifteen, was leaning down, drawing a wide circle around the clinic with a can of petrol.

"Please. Not the clinic."

"This is a government building. We must burn it down," he said, like he had been told to repeat this.

"It isn't," I said. He ignored me. "Just over there is a shebeen. Look, it's the one with the red sign. Lots of beer, break into that."

He looked up at me, eyes glazed.

My throat tightened with the grit from the smoke.

"Please, not this clinic," I said, touching his shoulders, touching the dangerous, petrol-soaked boy.

He got up, shrugging me off. "If you are lying about the

shebeen—" he dragged a finger across his neck.

I nodded. He whistled to the others, and they headed off to the tsotsi's shebeen.

Behind me, a handful of school children cheered.

A student with long beaded braids in red and yellow was suddenly at my shoulder. "We need water," she said.

Up ahead, thick black smoke was rising from other buildings.


## Zanele

"THE POLICE AREN'T HERE. COME," WINSTON SAID.

We turned out onto the street.

What Winston didn't say was that most of the streets were blocked by cars, students and tsotsi—and the students from Naledi, Jabavu and Morris Isaacson were leaning down into the windows of the cars and questioning the drivers before letting them pass. At the end of the street, students and tsotsi were breaking into the government building for Bantu affairs. Looting had spread to nearby shop fronts, grocery stores.

We walked onto Lembede Street. It was strangely quiet. Quiet because there were bullet holes in the shop fronts. One of the children picked up an exercise book from a school bag that lay spilled on the street.

A bicycle lay in the middle of the road, the wheel frame turned at an unnatural angle. Next to it, a lady's red hat, a wig and blood. Here and there, school blazers and small shoes. There was a smell too.

"They are probably in the hospital," Winston said, "or waiting to be buried."

I said nothing.

Winston pulled me by my shirt. "Keep walking. Fast."

THE PATH LEADING UP TO THE CHURCH WAS TRAMMELLED. Inside, hundreds of children were pressed against the ugly brick walls. Some children were being held by others, their bodies slack, like dolls. They looked up at us as we came in, but I avoided their eyes.

Some people were bringing water from the back of the church—I took some, washed dirt off my children and their cuts. Winston refused to take his bloody arm from under his shirt.

"There are too many of us in here," he said.

"What do you mean?"

"The police will come here."

"It's a church."

"You keep saying that."

"Where's your friend Tina?" I asked.

"Where's Vusi?"

The high walls of the church encircled us. Here was the painting that Billy had liked so much: black Madonna with baby Jesus, with machetes hidden in the background. In one hand, baby Jesus held the cross. His other hand made a victory sign.

"You know there aren't that many policemen in Soweto. But one of them can kill fifty of us easy. Pick us off like flies," Winston said after a while.

"They've come. They've killed us. What more can they do?"

"More will come. This is not finished."

"You're saying we should hit them first?"

I looked around at the hall, then back at Winston. We were weak. We were scattered. We were children. "I've hit a policeman before," I said. "It doesn't change anything. More will just keep coming."

He said nothing for a bit. Then, "You and Vusi were the ones who kept telling me that everything we do counts for something."

## Meena

WHEN I DID FIND THABO, IT WAS BY ACCIDENT. AND IT WAS not near the shebeen but on the grass of a park closer to Zanele's school. I recognized the fedora. It was a steel-grey silver one.

Thabo was the only Black Beret who got away with wearing a fedora.

I was looking for a bus to go back home. The mad old lady was still following me. I told her to go home, but she didn't seem to understand anything I said.

He was lying face down, his face sunk in what had been a flower bed. I turned him over. Someone had carved a line across his leg, up to his thigh. I leaned away and vomited. Past the bush, I saw abandoned placards, lost shoes and beanies. The old lady stepped in between me and the tsotsi, her eyes silently accusing.

Only when I thought to check did I realize that the tsotsi still had a faint pulse.

The old lady pointed, past Zanele's school. "We go there, now."

THEN THERE WAS A YOUNG BOY BEHIND US, CRAWLING OUT OF the bush, eyes fearful, a fresh jagged line across his cheek. His eyes on Thabo. "Is Thabo going to live?" he asked.

Slowly the boy, the old lady and I carried Thabo through the streets to a purple shack. There was a crowd outside, men with their hands in their overall pockets, looking at the sky. When they saw us, they became quiet and stared at the tsotsi.

The old lady's shack looked like it had once been cared for. We put the tsotsi on the only table in the room. His legs dangled off onto the floor. By now the old lady was covered in blood. As soon as she put him down, she stared, waiting for me to do something.

A thin boy came in, wearing what looked like a tattered

blue bathrobe. He looked at the old lady, the tsotsi and me. His face looked bleached, strangely old.

"You can't keep Thabo here," he said in a cold flat voice.

"Why? She brought us here."

"Can't you see the tsotsi stabbed him? They'll come back here looking for him."

"Okay," I said. "But I need something to wrap his wounds."

## Zanele

THE ALTAR GLEAMED CLEAN AND WHITE BEHIND ALL THE children. We sat with our knees against our chests.

Then a tear gas canister crashed through the ceiling. Then shards of glass. Then the smell of burning.

My eyes stung—I tore a strip of cloth off my shirt and pressed it onto my eyelids. Hands passed me plastic buckets of water to toss onto the canister.

The smell settled, then slowly faded. A cheer went up, bouncing off the high walls.

I took the cloth off my face. That's when I realized I couldn't see. I didn't see the policemen enter the church—only heard the disconnected shots against the walls, the altar.

Our bodies trapped each other in place. There were a few screams and then shots, then silence. I didn't scream. The bullets would have found me.

Nobody move, a policeman shouted.

The air in the church was cold and sweaty. People ran past and over my feet.

Then I felt someone take my hand and lead me outside, dragging me along as we ran, rocks sharp under my thin-soled shoes, more shots. We ran and ran, and all I had was the hand that pulled me along.

I began to see the blurred outlines of things. The tear gas was wearing off. Winston was next to me. No children. I took my hand out of his.

Winston said, "They cannot come here and shoot us like sheep."

"They just did." I put my hands on my knees and waited to get my breath back.

"They'll send the Special Branch now—they're trained to kill. These ones were just playing around."

"Yes."

I stood up—the sky was thick and grey. Behind me, a path was cut in the grass from the church. Made by the students who had managed to get away.

"We can try stop them," he said. "I know the route they'll take."

"What other choice do we have?"

## Meena

THE BOY IN THE BATHROBE TOLD ME THERE WAS A PHONE UP the street in a clothing shop. That's about as far as his help went, even with Thabo lying there bleeding.

I found the store mostly empty except for a couple of children rummaging through shirts and drinking beer from bottles with broken off tops. They looked up, not interested to know who I was or why I was there. I walked past them and dialled Jack's number, and waited for the call to connect.

"Hello, Craven residence?"

A woman picked up.

"Order for Jack Craven, for two hundred Chappies."

His mother's voice was clipped and thin. "I'm sorry, I think you've—"

"Ma'am. I am sure. I have the receipt here."

"Darling, there's this strange—"

I imagined a room, large oak cabinets and tall ceilings. I suddenly felt nauseous again.

"Hello?" Jack said, his voice strangely immediate. "Meena? I thought it was you, going on about Chappies. Is everything all right?"

"I don't know," I said. I took a breath and sighed into the phone.

"What's going on?" His voice had lost its friendliness now, even though he didn't, couldn't possibly know that Zanele was somewhere out there, amidst the shots, the burning buildings. And I was with the tsotsi. I felt weighed down by all the things I couldn't explain.

"It's bad. I need you to come with your car," I said, and told him where we were.

## Zanele

THE SPECIAL RIOT POLICE UNIT CAME IN SEVENTEEN VANS. The people behind us pushed us forward. Hundreds of us pouring onto the road, children in primary school, high school students, also tsotsis. Some carried the covers of dustbins as shields.

The outlines of the vans became clearer. They slowed as they came closer, then stopped—our bodies pressed against the sides of the vans. Hands slapped against their fenders.

Winston and I pushed past little children and some students from Orlando West. I pressed my face against the back window. In the back seat were three long rifles, with eyepieces attached to the top.

In the front were two men in khaki uniforms. The one

closest to us was bearded and looked like he was in his forties. He was saying something to his partner.

I tried the handle of his door. The man turned to look at me—his irises were thin and rimmed with grey. No fear in them. And then there were hands next to me and behind me, trying to get to the door. Then stones against the glass. Then our hands were on him, pulling him out.

He tried to throw us off, but there were many of us on him. We pushed him to the ground, and he sank down between the school shoes and bare feet. His cap had fallen off, a small balding spot exposed. That was the last I saw of the Special Branch policeman—the police emblem on his breast smeared with blood, his large powerful body flailing against us, our black arms pounding his flesh.

And then our cheers.

Soon police came, shouting, pushing past.

Then the scent of petroleum rose and hung between us. Students had come, carrying cans of petroleum.

Then I was pushed back.

I saw a black hand rise high in the air, holding a roll of burning newspaper like a torch. Everyone pushed forward when they saw the flame.

Later, the newspapers would say he was a celebrated commander who had served in Angola, one of their best. The flame rose and dipped down. And we shouted.

# SIXTEEN

## Jack

I SHOULD HAVE LISTENED TO THE RADIO THAT DAY. OR switched on the television. Maybe I would have caught on then, half an hour before I did.

After Meena's phone call, I looked at my watch. It was two in the afternoon. I picked up my father's newspaper off the breakfast table, but there was nothing in the paper, not yet.

I put down the newspaper, walked outside and started the car. The roads were quiet.

When I was halfway to Soweto, the traffic started slowing. Up ahead, the line of cars had broken, and students choked the street and the gaps between the scattered cars.

They came toward me in a thick connected mass. Their uniforms and their skin pressing against the metal surfaces of the car. They rapped their knuckles against the car windows, again and again.

I wound my window down—they could kill me if they wanted to anyway.

The boy at the window closest to me put his face inside. He was wearing the dark blue and black of Zanele's school.

The boy took my face in his hand and turned it so I had to look at him directly. "Mlungu," he said. "What are you doing here?" The sweat on his hand was cold.

I didn't answer. My mind was wandering up and down the crowded road, the dust, the smoke, the torn flaps of shirts.

"Where is Zanele?" I said in a quiet voice.

The boy leaned in farther. "What did you say? Speak up." His voice rose, sharpened. His fingers were strong, the tips of them sinking into my throat.

"Please," I said, choking. Slowly, the boy let go of my throat.

"Give us black power, mlungu," he said, and he held his fist up, the thumb in front. "I want to see your fist held high or we will take you out of your car."

I held my fist up. And slowly the bodies parted. It was easy.

I STOPPED OUTSIDE THE SHACK WITH THE PURPLE-PAINTED front that Meena had described. Then I went inside. There was a bloody figure on a rickety low table. The face was turned away. It wasn't Zanele.

"Where is she?" I said.

Meena was adding a layer of torn fabric onto the gangster's leg. Another boy came in, wearing an unwashed coat.

"Who?" he said.

In the corner of the room was an old lady with the hair on one side of her head sticking up. The front of her dress was spattered with blood. The old lady opened her mouth, but no sound came out.

"Zanele?" I said to the boy.

He didn't answer.

"I called to see if you could pick up Thabo," Meena said. "These people don't want him here."

I stared at the dust in her hair, and on the silly, oversized hand-me-down uniform she was wearing. "You called me because Zanele needed help."

"I said I didn't know," Meena said. "I didn't even mention her name. Zanele is probably somewhere out there. If you let Thabo die, she will be angry."

"You lied just to save your gangster," I said in a slow deliberate voice, to make sense of things. "We need to find Zanele."

"He is not my gangster," she said. Then, "What do you want me to do? Go running out on the street yelling her name?"

"When did you last hear from her?"

"Yesterday. Seemed excited, told me something was going to happen today. So I came here. Didn't know it was this."

I turned back to the car.

"We need your help," Meena said.

"I don't think you understand. I don't give a damn about your gangster."

That's when we heard the police helicopters coming. They rose from behind a set of buildings and hovered above us. People came out of their shacks next door, and stared.

"She probably didn't know this was going to happen," Meena replied. The front of her uniform was bloody.

MEENA OPENED THE BACK DOOR OF THE CAR AND, WITH THE help of the old woman and the boy, put the gangster inside. His face was less bloodied than the rest of his body, and the expression on it was slack and childlike.

I started the engine. The boy and the old lady watched us from in front of their shack.

"Let's go to the clinic first. We need to fetch some supplies. Come, I'll show you the way. The only thing is, where do we hide him?"

"Hide him?"

"Yes," she said, impatient. "I'm sure you know a place."

MY FATHER'S WAREHOUSE HAD HIGH CEILINGS AND WAS MUCH larger than his failed business needed. Walls of unopened blue-labelled bottles rose in the dim light, and the place smelled of dust. My father had fired the supervisor and left the warehouse empty till he could "pin down" his orders. We set him down in a space next to the back wall. Meena unwrapped the cloth over his wounds and set out the medical supplies. I cleared boxes of beer and stacked them in higher piles to create a barrier between the body and the door on the far right.

Meena looked up from cutting a bandage. "You're going to try and go back there to find her, aren't you?"

I didn't reply.

"I am going to make sure Thabo doesn't die," Meena said. "So pick me up around eight."

I didn't bother telling her about how the gangster had gone for me and my car.

I DIDN'T FIND ZANELE. THE ROADS INTO THE TOWNSHIP WERE blocked by the kids or the police, and amandla didn't cut it anymore. Later in the afternoon, a policeman leaned heavily against the ledge of my window. His breath smelled of beer.

"Go back, my friend, go back."

"My sister is in there, sir. With the Christian Homes Charity. She came this morning to give out blankets. I need to find her."

"That's unfortunate, sir. Our force is doing our best to secure the area."

"I'm not asking your opinion on the situation. I'm asking you to let me in."

The man shrugged, slapped my car as if to bid it on its way.

I tried again and again, wide circles around the township, but there was no way in, and it got darker. I'll hear from her. That's what I told myself as I drove back to the beer warehouse.

THREE DAYS LATER, I READ IN THE *RAND DAILY* THAT THE FIRST boy to die was not Hector Pieterson, a skinny fifteen-year-old, but someone called Hastings Ndlovu.

I read all the newspapers, pieced together a chronology of events. M.C. Botha's education policy, about teaching all subjects in Afrikaans, hadn't gone down well with the students. Hadn't gone down well for some time. The pamphlets. Those empty schools. From everywhere in Soweto, they organized a mass protest. They were supposed to meet in Orlando Stadium.

They never made it that far.

The students from Zanele's school marched out onto Mputhi Road and collected others from Theseli and Naledi. They walked from the township onto the bridge. Then at the bridge, police started shooting. And the students scattered.

First the papers made a big deal about a police dog that was killed by the crowd. "Savage," the report said.

But the main story came a few days after that. The headline POLICEMAN BRUTALLY MURDERED was paired with a picture of a charred military van, with the blurred image of a burned body.

I left the television on, watching the repeated minute-long clips of police holding off the crowd, throwing tear-gas canisters into the masses of students.

I SHOULD HAVE KNOWN WHAT ZANELE WAS PLANNING, EVEN IF she'd made it a condition that I never ask. That condition had seemed easy to accept, then.

A week, and Zanele still hadn't been found. My mother gave Lillian three days off to look for her. Maybe because she believed in a mother's right to bury her daughter—even if the mother was the help.

But there was no sign of her. I drove into Soweto every morning around ten. I went, even when it became less likely she was alive.

There were no estimates in the papers for how many had died. No names either, except Hector and Hastings.

But there would be arrest records. So, a week after Zanele had gone missing, I came back from my circling, useless driving and rang Oliver to ask for his father's office number. He kept asking me why I hadn't answered his calls. When I finally got the number, I hung up and dialled Oliver's father.

"Colonel Joubert. Morning."

"Ah," he said, a note of amusement in his voice. "Who is this?"

"You know it's me," I said. "And I've called to tell you that I'm ready to—what do you people call it? Give a statement."

"Confess," Colonel Joubert spat out.

"Whatever makes you happy," I said.

"Jack, my boy, I appreciate it," Joubert said. "I appreciate it, really. And I would be happy to take your statement personally. But right at this moment I am busy."

"With the Soweto riot arrests? I understand. But I think you'll see that my statement is very relevant." I put down the phone before he could reply.

I put on a checked cardigan bought in England and a pair of black trousers. I stopped at the small crucifix on the mantelpiece. I hoped, tried to pray, that Zanele was in the arrest records. But I'd never been very religious.

"You just can't wait to leave, can you?" My mother stopped me at the door. She ran her fingers over the cardigan, smoothing it over, a false cheery note in her voice.

"Yes," I said, and went outside. By the weeping willow, a few ibis pecked at the yellow grass. There was a burned, bitter smell in air, probably from the neighbours' cooking.

I took a quick turn to the left, to the maid quarters. I walked into Lillian's room without knocking. She looked up slowly from her meal of rice and chicken gizzards.

"Do you know where Zanele is?"

Lillian's face didn't change.

"You must realize what you are doing—what you're going to make me do if you don't answer. I'm going to the police to see if she's been arrested. Get us both into trouble." I stepped closer. "I need to know she's alive. Do you understand?"

"You must learn some manners," Lillian said. Her voice was deeper, more gravelly than I'd remembered. She spoke so little now that I was surprised by the sound of her voice. For a moment I recognized Zanele's face, then it was gone.

"Maybe you're right," I said. "But I need to know if she is alive."

Lillian put the tray of food aside and got up from her bed. "Wait and listen to what someone is saying before you talk."

I waited. Lillian began to pack away her lunch in foil.

"I'm going to the police," I said.

"This is not your business. She is my daughter."

I turned and left.

## SEVENTEEN

## Meena

THABO GOT BETTER, AND THIS SURPRISED ME, BECAUSE I LEFT him for hours alone in the warehouse with nothing, a glass of water and sometimes bread or roti from our kitchen. When he first regained consciousness, he seemed to recognize me. After looking unpleasantly surprised at seeing me, he came to accept the bandages, my feeding him and not answering his questions about Zanele.

Jack had given me the keys and only occasionally agreed to drive me, which meant I had to ask Dr A. to take me after clinic.

Jack would call from public telephones. The police were already onto him, he said, but he didn't explain why. He would call and ask about Zanele. When I said I had nothing, he would hang up. I remembered how he'd been at the shop, friendly in the careless, intimate way that charming people are.

The more he called to ask about her, the more Zanele ceased to become a question. I wanted to say a lot of things to Jack then. What had he really expected from starting a relationship with Zanele? Sometimes I wanted to tell him to shut up, stop calling.

I kept going over the last time I'd seen her. Zanele, excited, rolling a tube of lipstick on the counter. The shade of lipstick was a loud, unlikely red.

I knew this was the part of me that hadn't recovered from what had happened—the tsotsi's body heavy and still on the grass. Reading about the police shootings in *The Sowetan*. So I said as little as possible.

JONAS CAME IN ONE AFTERNOON, ONE OF THOSE DAYS WHEN I'd talked to both Thabo and Jack, listened to them both replay the events of that afternoon in microscopic detail. Listened to Thabo's persistent, repeated questions about Zanele.

Jonas' baas had lent him his television for the weekend. Could I believe it? His own television.

"Yes, he's letting you get a few soapies in before you die of TB." My voice was flat and cold.

Jonas stopped in mid flow about the shows and music on the television.

"He knows you're dying, Jonas. And he's not doing a thing to help you, just feeding you more cigarettes so you die sooner." And then suddenly, too late, I realized what I'd done. "Sorry. Jonas. I'm sorry."

He sat there, blinking slowly in the dim light of the shop. I made him tea, and we continued the conversation like I hadn't just told him he was going to die.

AT THE CLINIC, DR A. AND I STITCHED AND MENDED AND sent people away when supplies ran out. Afterward, I looked after Thabo as if doing that would bring Zanele back. I knew it made no sense, but that's all I had.

At the shop, I became careless, missed shifts and money. Whatever Papa said mattered less than the blood and the mending in the township. Many times I lost track of what he was saying, what he was trying to say. I wanted to tell him that I was going to leave the shop, leave school. It didn't make sense anymore, when the police just shot children and left them to die in the street.

THABO NEVER SPOKE TO ME. HIS EYES JUST FIXED ON MY FACE whenever I changed the dressing. Occasionally he leaned up on his elbows and, with a finger, poked the skin sewn together on his thigh.

Of course I didn't tell him that I'd sent those boys to raid his shebeen.

One day when I came in, he was limping up and down the warehouse in his torn shirt.

"Zanele?" he asked.

"We don't know," I said.

I knew then that I would feel worse without having the tsotsi to look after.

"We?" he asked.

"The white guy, Jack," I said. "You're in his warehouse right now."

He clicked his tongue against his teeth. He was taking this better than I expected, maybe because he had suspected it for some time, walking around the cases of beer.

"This was your idea?" he asked, gesturing to the beer.

"No, his."

Thabo walked up to me, looking me up and down. For a moment I thought he might thank me for saving his life.

"Dr A. has his car parked down the road," I said.

"Now you tell me." He brushed past me to the back door of the warehouse, past the metal mesh gate. I locked the warehouse door behind us, and followed.


## Thabo

First, I needed a new shirt, and I went to the shop with Meena so that she could get one for me from the men's shelf. They were not the best, but at least they were new.

"Why can't you go home and get one?" she asked in the car. Dr A. looked at us in the rear-view mirror and said nothing.

"You're scared of showing up in the township, aren't you?" Meena said. "They want you dead." She seemed to remember something suddenly, and fell silent.

In the end I had to wait at the back of the shop for Meena to get one of her father's old shirts, an ugly, loose, grey-checked one that even her father didn't want.

"You're not even trying," Meena said, and came forward to pull the collar out. I moved back, and Meena took her hands away.

That was stupid—she'd stitched me up. She was looking after tsotsis like they were her problem.

Everything was changed. A mlungu was giving me shelter, an Indian girl was straightening my collar like she was my mother, my Black Berets wanted me dead, and Zanele was gone.

"We haven't heard anything for a week now," Meena said, when I asked about Zanele. "I'm telling you the truth."


## Jack

WHEN I KNOCKED ON THE DOOR OF HIS OFFICE ON THE THIRD floor of the station, Joubert took his time to respond. I heard him clear his throat a few times. Then he told me to come in. I sat down before he had a chance to tell me to. The chair sloped a little forward, as if I was supposed to feel like I was crouching, kneeling in front of him.

Joubert's office looked out on the Carlton Hotel and the Standard Bank Building. There were no framed pictures of Oliver here. A paperweight from Anglo American and one from Sasol sat on either side of his desk.

"How've you been, my boy?" Joubert asked, scratching his beard. It made an unpleasant sound.

Judging by the stack of reports piled next to him, it looked like Joubert was pressed for time. Vorster and his cabinet were breathing down his neck about the riots—and here he was, wasting time with me.

"You should have looked into my statistical model idea," I said.

"Your idea?" Joubert continued scratching his beard, but slower now. The conversation had taken a turn he hadn't planned for.

"The statistical model that predicts civilian unrest. The one I told you about at dinner."

Joubert smiled at me indulgently. "Yes, very clever," he said, his eyes turning to the clock.

There were still hundreds of students on the loose, more riots breaking out across the country.

"Her name is Zanele," I said. "Zanele Mthembu."

Joubert blinked at me.

"It's spelled Z-a-n-e-l-e."

Still nothing.

"In case you want to look it up in that file of yours. I'm assuming you have a file on people like her. One of their leaders."

## Meena

I GOT A CALL AT AROUND TWO IN THE AFTERNOON.

"It's done," Jack said.

"What?" I said. The line buzzed, then became clear.

"I told the police. So now they know her name. Now I know for a fact they haven't got her in jail."

"You went to the police. Are you crazy?"

"He checked."

"He?"

"Joubert. He's a colonel in the police."

"Why would he do that?"

"He wanted to get to me. He said there's no sign of her, she's probably dead."

"You know a colonel?"

"You're focusing on the wrong thing here." Jack's voice took on an edge.

It was a symptom of his nerves. He had probably never lost anyone before.

"But there's also a chance she's on the run, there are plenty of them, the tsotsi even—"

"She must be dead," Jack said, and hung up, the click loud.

THABO DIDN'T THINK SHE WAS DEAD, AND GOT FIERCE IF YOU even suggested it. But Jack didn't have the tsotsi to talk to. And what did Thabo know anyway?

Still, there were many bodies waiting to be claimed and buried.

Jack didn't call for a while after that.

I cried once for Zanele. Her life seemed to be, from the first moment I'd met her, a series of events leading to her death. And I missed her.

Often my grandmother came to my room and scolded me. To Papa I said nothing. Papa didn't know any of this, and could hardly be expected to understand what this felt like, how I read the faces outside the shop window.

There was the clinic. But there were only so many supplies. We did our best there. But we couldn't change what had happened.

# Thabo

STILL THE SHEBEEN WASN'T FIXED. PIECES OF THE ROOF AND broken glass were all over the street.

I understood why Lerato had stabbed me. Sizwe wanted me dead for the missing money. He didn't take kak, even when the rest of Soweto was burning.

Getting stabbed by your own gang was the worst thing that could happen to a tsotsi.

It was good that Sizwe believed I was dead. He wouldn't be looking for me, definitely not in Zanele's baba's old mining uniform. I only went out around dawn, when the Berets would be sleeping.

It was hard to hide in a place where everyone knew you.

The uniform was too big for me, but I didn't say anything, because Mankwe wasn't in the mood for jokes. She just kept walking up and down in the space between Zanele's mattress and the bathtub piled on all those bricks they'd collected. There were only three steps from one side to the other.

Zanele had been gone for more than two weeks now. Mankwe had looked in all the usual places. The bush boys, Masi, Vusi were gone. Mankwe had asked where the rest were hiding—but there were so many police everywhere, so many people in jail; anyone you asked suspected you were an informer.

The police had been looking for Masi every day. I'd heard that he was hiding here by pretending to be a girl. But then all those bored kids with no school, they would say anything to pass the time.

Then Mankwe started thinking Zanele was dead.

There were a few pieces of coal left in the bag. I took them outside the shack and lit them.

"I'm getting water," I told Mankwe, and left the shack for

the well. I thought a bath and eating some hot paap would make her feel better.

As I turned back from the well and carried the water up the hill, I saw them. I dropped the bucket and ran, but I was too late. Inside were five policemen, stepping all over Zanele's mattress.

They never brought so many abo gata to arrest just one person. One of them had a clipboard and a pen. He was waving a photograph in Mankwe's face. Another two held Mankwe, who had handcuffs around her wrists. She was looking straight ahead. The others just stood around.

I stopped at the door. "This is a mistake," I said. "She did nothing." They pushed past me. And then I said what Zanele would have wanted me to say. "She is not Zanele. You have the wrong person."

One of them hit me with the back of his gun. I fell. One of them stepped on my hand.

"She killed one of the ours, you fokking *kaffir*. She's going to get moered for this." I heard a car door open and close. Then he took his boot off my hand, and left.

Mankwe believed that Zanele was alive. There was no other reason for her to let them take her away.

## EIGHTEEN

## Jack

I DROVE AROUND FOR THE NEXT FEW DAYS, SPENDING THE nights drinking beer with Ricky and watching television with the sound off.

Ricky didn't ask many questions, maybe because I chose not to answer them.

It seemed Joubert still hadn't told Oliver or anyone else about Zanele and me, which was mildly surprising. Whenever Oliver came by to visit Ricky, I left.

But one time, Oliver caught me at home. "Pa says I can't be friends with you anymore. Says you're disturbed. "

I kept staring at the television. "You should listen to him."

"Tell me what happened."

"No."

"Why?"

"Because in some ways you are no different than your Pa," I said.

"Screw you, Jack," Oliver said, his ears red. Then he left.

LILLIAN STOPPED WORKING AT OUR HOUSE A FEW DAYS LATER. My mother had been complaining about her slow shuffling, the dirty counters. She didn't mention her dead daughter, of course.

Zanele's death hung between me and everyone else, my mother, Ricky, my parents. Only Lillian knew—the way she would lower her eyes when I came into the room, so I couldn't see the anger and the grief.

My mother made phone calls. A new maid came in who talked more than Lillian.

MEENA CALLED. "HER SISTER WAS ARRESTED. HAPPY?"
"What do you mean?"
"The police came and arrested her."
"I don't—"
Then Meena hung up. I'd been cut off from my only link to Zanele.

THE POLICE COULDN'T FIND ZANELE, SO THEY ARRESTED HER sister. I wasn't surprised.

I started smoking my father's cigarettes, taking them out of his desk drawer. We'd sit together on the porch. The embers crumbled gold and then black as we flicked our stubs in the ashtray.

"Oxford," my father said. "Your mother reckons it will make you feel better when you're away from here."

"Yes," I said. "I'm sorry, I've no idea why I'm acting this way."

My father didn't say anything for a while then. "You know my warehouse? Broken into. Overnight, cleaned out of my entire stock of Trident."

"What are you going to do now?"

"There's no insurance on it, Jack. There's nothing in hell I can do." He ground his cigarette into the flower bed, as my mother always told him not to. "Jack, you can't get shot to pieces. Not now." He walked back inside, and I wondered how he managed that faint trace of irritation in his voice.

IN LOW VOICES, I HEARD THEM TALKING ABOUT ME. "OLIVER and he don't speak anymore. And he hasn't even talked to Megan. She says they broke up suddenly. I don't know what to do, James. I just don't know why he's acting like this."

## Meena

It was ten on a Saturday morning. Papa was doing the bills upstairs. The shop phone rang and I picked it up. "Pillay's All Purpose. How may I help you? Hello?"

No reply on the phone. Just a breath, then another one.

"Hello."

"I need a place to stay."

I knew the voice immediately. "Where've you been?"

"Hiding. What else? And, Meena?"

"Yes?"

"Don't tell anyone. Don't tell Jack."

Zanele peeled off layers of clothing in our storeroom, that old blue jacket, sweaters, an ugly brown-and-yellow beanie. Under it, her hair had been shaved off.

She was much thinner and if she noticed I was staring at her, the smallness of her, she didn't say.

"Papa will come in here to check things," I said. "Tomorrow he does stock taking."

"I know," she said. "I won't stay long."

I put my hands on her shoulders but didn't hug her, she looked too fragile for that. She closed her eyes. I went to the other side of the storeroom, opened cans of condensed milk and packets of biscuits. I put them down in front of her. She ate the biscuits, three at a time, crouched against the dusty wall of the storeroom. She tipped the can of milk to her mouth, wiping her lips off with her sleeve when she'd finished.

I decided not to tell her about Mankwe.

But then I did anyway. "Mankwe—"

"What about her?"

"The police have arrested her—instead of you."

Zanele lifted her head up slowly from the wall. Her eyes wandered around the room with its dark cans and dusty shelves, then settled on me.

"Thabo was there. They said you killed a policeman."

Zanele leaned her head back against the wall.

"Is it true?"

"Yes. Where did they take her?"

"Why?"

Zanele ignored my question. "When did this happen?"

"Two days ago. Mankwe didn't say she wasn't you."

Zanele got up, pulled on her beanie. And I thought she was going to go right then.

"I have a better idea," I said, running between her and the door.

She stopped. "Tell me quickly. In a minute, I go to the police station."


# Thabo

THE NEXT TIME I CAME TO THE SHOP, MEENA'S FATHER WAS facing her across the counter, looking angry. He was holding up a man's blue jacket that looked familiar. "Someone has been in our storeroom. Is anything missing?"

"No," Meena said.

Eish, the girl was bad at lying.

"You're sure, you've checked?"

I cleared my throat. "Give me two packs of cigarettes. Yes, that means you," I said, pointing at Meena. She looked irritated. I looked at the jacket. The number 729.

Meena passed them over and held out five rand.

The father turned to me. "That is ten rand minus five for the cigarettes. As per our agreement."

I waved off the money but took the cigarettes. "I don't need your people's money anymore," I said. "Baie dankie, meneer."

The father crossed his arms and frowned at me. Good for him.

Zanele was back, alive. Just like her to come to Meena first.

## Jack

I GOT THE CALL FROM MEENA LATE AFTERNOON. I PICKED UP the phone because my mother was out, and the new maid was not allowed to answer calls. I lifted the receiver, dangled it in my fingers. Then I put my ear to it.

"I told you not to call here," I said.

"Come to the shop," Meena said.

## Zanele

MEENA KEPT TELLING ME HER PLAN WOULD WORK. THAT THEY would release Mankwe. That this was safer. She was taking pictures of me with her father's old camera. This was part of the plan. I kept thinking of Mankwe, of the shack with Mama in it. Maybe she understood why Mankwe had done that for me, when I didn't.

But maybe Mankwe was already dead. After waiting outside the police station every day, we would be told she had died of influenza, she had slipped in the shower or she had thrown herself out the window.

Yesterday I got a message out to Mama and Thabo through Meena. It was short—I am alive.

I would wait three days, and then turn myself in if Mankwe wasn't released. That was our plan. I trusted her so much now. Maybe it was because she was all I had left.

I TRIED TO SLEEP, FACING THE HOLE IN THE WALL OF THE abandoned shack. Through the hole, you could see the dump, and the smell was everywhere. I started thinking of Jack instead. I imagined him eating breakfast on his patio, the kudu heads waiting on the dining room walls. I tried to imagine the flow of his thoughts, tricky—Jack rarely showed what he felt. I'd only seen pieces of him.

He probably thought I was dead.

And the dead policeman changed things even more—a policeman burned alive.

I could tell Jack that I pulled him out of the car but that the others dragged him away. Then someone came with the petrol and a lighter, and it just happened. I had to pull that policeman out of his car to stop him shooting us.

And that was all true.

Jack would list my actions like a sequence of logical points, and then pause, check if they made sense to him. And maybe they would. Maybe they wouldn't.

I could choose not to tell him how angry I was—how when I pulled the policeman out of the car, I wanted him dead.

It was better for it to end this way. We will never see each other again. That was the way it was meant to be.

## Jack

ACROSS THE COUNTER, MEENA HANDED ME AN ENVELOPE. "What's this?"

"*Rand Daily Mail* —you know their editor. Make sure he gets this."

I tossed the envelope back on the counter.

"It's for getting Zanele's sister free. But don't open it."

Meena reached forward to stop me, but I picked it up and

stepped back. Then I slipped the photograph out—Zanele with all her hair gone, holding up yesterday's paper, smiling. She was standing in front of a fruit stall. Zanele's signed statement, her passbook.

I slipped them back in the envelope. "Where is she?"

"It's not safe for you to know."

"I didn't get a message from her. Nothing."

"No one got a message."

"She's upstairs, isn't she? You've hidden her here." I went behind the counter and went up the steps, fast. I rounded the corner, opened the door—to her father. He looked up from his papers. His eyes blinked behind gold-rimmed glasses.

"Sir," he said. "Can I help you?"

## Meena

"THE POLICEMAN FROM THE PAPERS, THE ONE WHO DIED— it's true," I said.

Thabo shrugged.

I looked up from scanning the newspapers for a report on Mankwe's arrest. Nothing yet.

Thabo was wearing a new suit. He was back to walking around like he owned the streets. I didn't ask how he'd done it. He looked out the shop door and flipped the sign to CLOSED. "We need to get her out of here."

"She can't stay with me, my father will find out."

"I mean across the border, domkop."

"How do you plan to do that?"

"I have some money. And I know who to talk to." Thabo dismissed me with his hands. "I just need time."

"These people—" I leaned forward and whispered, "—are they ANC?"

"They aren't hard to find."

"How do I help?"

"You pass messages, you don't get caught. Otherwise—"
Thabo slid a finger across his throat.

"Oh, please."

"You be careful."

"So if we get her out," I said, folding over the paper, "what
about me?"

"What do you mean, what about you?" Thabo looked at
me like I was crazy. "You concentrate on this plan. Nothing
else. Nothing. I will have it all ready in three days. You tell
her." He took his cigarettes and left.

If the tsotsi didn't understand that I wanted to go with
Zanele, no one would.

But there was nothing left for me here.

NINETEEN

## Jack

"I'M SURPRISED YOU CALLED." MEGAN PUT HER PURSE ON THE table.

My mother, fidgeting, placed a tray of biscuits and fruit juice in front of us like we were back in prep school. Then she retreated.

"Let's go into the garden," I said.

"Okay." She followed me out onto the patio. Shafts of light glinted on the tiles. I stepped out onto the grass. It crackled underfoot. The gardener hadn't come for a few weeks. I walked to the weeping willow, the old slide and swing set.

I took the envelope from my jacket pocket and handed it to Megan. She slid out the pictures, the letter, the passbook. "I need you to take that to your dad. He needs to make it public—the police jailed the wrong person."

"I don't understand."

"Read the letter, it explains most of it."

Megan brought the pictures closer. There was something startling about Zanele's smile, it looked as if she was about to laugh. And I didn't believe it. "Who is this?"

"You can talk to Oliver's dad, he'll tell you about it. The Immorality Act case that links me to her."

Still Megan didn't say anything, her eyes fixed on my face.

"If you have the convictions you keep talking about, you will do this," I said. "That's it. That's all I wanted to say." And then I turned back to the house.

I could have apologized to her for all of this, but I didn't. She would've disliked me more for it, I think.

NEXT I DROVE TO RICKY'S HOUSE. THE DRIVEWAY TO THEIR place was long, littered with his mother's attempts at trees. Stunted branches that had lost their leaves sat next to fat evergreens.

Ricky was in a deckchair next to the covered pool. A Harvard sweater over his stocky body, his eyes closed, his fingers laced behind his head. He opened his eyes slowly, like he'd been sleeping, even though he'd accepted the call to let me in.

"Jacky," he said. There was a note of affection in his voice. Maybe I'd only noticed it now. He probably liked the recent version of me better, the one that said nothing and sat with him in the dark, and drank.

"Your parents have a house up by Magaliesburg," I said.

Nothing.

"Can I have the keys?"

Ricky adjusted his position on the deckchair, squinted up at me. "Sure thing, Jacky, but, like any normal person would ask, why?"

"It's better you don't know."

"Better I don't know," Ricky repeated, pretending to consider the words.

"And better to say nothing. Even if people ask questions."

"It isn't like you to hold me to things like that, you know."

"Just give me the keys."

"You're not acting rationally. I hope you know that."

"Are you giving them to me or not?"

"If I give you the keys, something is going to happen. It better end whatever meltdown you've been going through these last few days. You're becoming boring."

"I need the keys now."

"Easy, boy, easy." He got up from the deckchair, slowly. He sighed and went inside the house, the dirty soles of his bare feet marking the beige carpet. The back of his mullet haircut untidy.

## Zanele

THE SOUND OF THE ENGINE WAS POWERFUL, A SLOW thrumming sound. I could hear it from down the street. It was coming for me.

I skirted to the back of the shack and waited on the side that faced the dump.

The car stopped. Then started again. I waited.

I saw it come up on the small dirt track, a wide-breasted silver car, the interior dark. I started running. Boots against the gravel on the road.

"Zanele."

I stopped and turned.

I looked at the shack again. The rusted walls were curved inward, bending but not cracking. My eyes lingered there, at the eaves. Then I looked at him. I had forgotten how pale he was, had forgotten how some of the lines of his face were like his mother's.

"That isn't your car," I said.

"Meena gave me the pictures to get your sister released."

"Of course she did."

"Meena told me a lot of things." His hair was uncombed and the top buttons of his shirt were undone.

"So?"

Jack tossed the car keys in his hand and gestured toward the car. He got inside and I stood there, the gleaming metal between us.

"You need to tell me what's been going on—you owe me that much," he said.

I got inside. "Why don't we talk about you first. What's new with the Cravens?"

## Meena

"See? They printed it. Now it's only a matter of time till they release Mankwe."

Thabo snatched the paper and looked at the picture. "Where's Zee?"

"Safe. Everything set for tomorrow night at eleven?"

"Yes, wena. And not so loud." He tossed the paper on the counter. "Where is she? Tell me."

"With the mlungu, I think." I scanned his face. His expression didn't change. "She wouldn't go with him if she didn't want to. You can't be making the plan and making sure she's safe. I told her where and when to meet."

"Learn something," he said at last. It was the tsotsi's voice, threatening, impersonal. "Be quiet when you make a mistake."

I thought he would break things. Just the sound of his shoes across the shop floor until he swung the door open and left.

## Thabo

It was bad luck that just after I came back from the shop, Sam Shenge, with his best green bow tie, was waiting in the shebeen.

It was bad luck that he said, "Thabo, you have something for me?"

"*Gaan blaas,*" I said.

He didn't go anywhere, asked me to get him another beer. "I know there's a package going to Swaziland, going through here," he said. "A package that the abo gata won't like."

"Why are you calling them abo gata? You're just like them."

"So are you, my friend, so are you. So tell me. Where is that girlfriend of yours?"

"Why don't you ask her mlungu?"

"Her mlungu?" Sam asked.

"I have nothing to tell you."

"You never have."

"Drink it and leave. And don't come back here."

"You can say what you want, my friend." Sam stepped away from his glass of beer. "But the abo gata rule Soweto. You tsotsi just like to pretend."

# Jack

I STOPPED THE CAR IN FRONT OF RICKY'S HOUSE. I WENT around to her side of the car, but she'd opened the door already and was standing, looking up at the French windows on the second floor. A stream wove itself around the house.

She looked thinner. I wanted to hold her, but I walked past and unlocked the door. She followed me in, and we faced each other across the kitchen counter.

Outside, the last flecks of sunlight on the branches and her face.

"I went to the police to find out if you were in jail. They know about us. You know that."

"Then they'll find me here."

"They won't look here."

Zanele turned away and looked out the window. Dry bush and grass pressed against the glass. A three-hour drive separated us from the city and the police.

"There's a bedroom upstairs, on the right. You can sleep there," I said, turning away.

"They're taking me across the border tomorrow. You know that?" she said, coming up behind me. She pulled my shoulder and turned me around. "You're angry."

"I thought the police had buried you, and you let me believe that."

"So why did you bring me here?"

HOURS LATER, I PUT SOME PASTA FROM THE STORAGE CUPBOARD on the stove and added some sauce. I brought it up to Zanele's bedroom, nudging the door open with my shoulder. I found her curled up on top of the sheets. Her breathing was slow and uneven.

I put the bowl down on the chest of drawers next to the bed. Then I took the gun I had taken from my father's study from its holster and put it next to the bowl.

I put my hand on her head, where all her hair had been shaved off. It was bristly and uneven. She shifted, opened her eyes and looked at the gun.

"Why do you think I didn't tell you?"

"Tell me," I said.

"It was cleaner that way," Zanele said, leaning up against the headboard. "You go to England, I go to Swaziland. No goodbyes, that's it." For a moment I glimpsed something pleading in her expression. She wanted me to let go.

"That's not how these things work," I said. "And I'm still angry."

"I know." She moved her face away from my hand and sunk back into bed.

"Here's some food."

"I'll have it later."

"I've been reading the papers more," I said. "Seems like your riot started something. It's all over the country. And it looks like Botha is backing down on the Afrikaans."

"It's just the beginning," she said. "It's not enough. It was never just about Afrikaans."

"Of course not."

"The thing about the policeman," she said after a while.

"It's true. I pulled him out of his car with my own hands. I killed him."

"You killed him?"

"I pulled him out of the car and then he was burned alive."

"So the mob got him. Your bunch of students."

"Yes."

"So you didn't kill him yourself."

"Does it make a difference?"

"It's strange that you want to take credit for killing him."

"If you think I'm sorry he died, I'm not."

"Of course not. You couldn't care less. He is mlungu."

"So are you."

I didn't say anything. I leaned back in the chair and waited for her to fall asleep. But she didn't. She took my collar and pulled me toward her. And I let her.

# TWENTY

## Zanele

IT WAS ALMOST MORNING NOW. LIGHT FELL ON THE CREAM sheets, the thick mattress. Jack was still asleep. I picked up his shirt and put it on. I thought about my mother standing against the light, making her braids.

"That shirt looks good on you," Jack said, his voice sleepy, unworried. He reached out, pulled me down onto the bed, kissing me, and it was like all the times before, but different too.

"Come with me to England," he said. "I'll find a way to get you there."

"You know I won't—"

"—too far."

"Yes."

"I know you care I'm leaving," he said. "I know you do."

"Yes," I said, my eyes resting on his.

"So?"

"It can't be helped."

"Can't be helped?" He put his arms around me, rested his face against my shoulder.

We had a few hours, at most.

WHEN I WOKE UP, A MLUNGU WAS SITTING ON THE CHAIR staring at Jack's hand, which was resting on the sheet that covered me. Jack's friend. He was broad and had light reddish hair.

On the night table, the gun, but Jack's friend wasn't looking at that.

"I don't think we've met," he said. "Ricky."

"We have," I said.

"You have a name?"

"You must have had a long drive."

"Not too bad. You liking the house?"

"It's yours?"

"Yes."

"Thanks for lending it."

"Pleasure. I didn't see this coming. Jack's a sly one."

"I'm sure," I said.

"Get out, Ricky," Jack said, in a low angry voice.

"You can't trust him," Ricky continued. "Jack always keeps a couple of girls on the line. We don't know how he does it."

"Get the hell out, Ricky."

Ricky shrugged, stumbled out of the room.

"Will he tell anyone we're here?" I said.

But Jack put his trousers on and left the room, after Ricky, after things that didn't matter. I heard his raised voice through the next room.

A few hours till I met Thabo. And the police between me and the Swaziland border.

But I didn't have to wait that long for them to find me.


# Meena

THE PHONE RANG AND I PICKED UP.

"The Special Branch. Coetzee. He's come for me."

"Zanele? Where are you?"

But she was gone. I put the phone down slowly.

Jonas walked into the shop. His body was stooped over, like he was collapsing onto himself. He picked Zanele's jacket off the stool and sat down.

He turned the jacket over in his hands. "I like this jacket," he said. "I had one like this." He stared at the logo on the back.

"Maybe it's yours," I said impatiently, my nails tapping at the till, waiting for him to leave.

"No," he said slowly. "I left mine with my wife and I never went back for it."

I looked behind Jonas for any sign of Thabo. He was meant to come and confirm everything with me. He was supposed to come.

"She told me never to come back," he said.

One of Thabo's boys walked by the shop window and I gestured to him—my hand, slicing across my neck. The boy nodded, ran off.

"She took my children, she got everything. Anyway, they were girls. They would end up like her. So I left them with her. Ha. Some women are like stones—even in the storm, the cold, the fire, they survive. Yes I had two girls. Mankwe was the pretty one. We named the younger one Zanele. In Zulu, we call the last daughter Zanele. The name gives us luck so we get a son the next time. But we got no son."

I took the jacket from Jonas and stared at it. I looked up at him, at the reddened, unhealthy whites of his eyes. "You left them. Your girls," my voice shook. "Now, today. Today your baas is going to kill Zanele. And Mankwe is in jail."

Jonas coughed. "Two Lucky Strikes, from the shelf, *asseblief.*"

"The name of your wife is Lillian, isn't it?" I said, not moving from the counter. "Coetzee has Mankwe. And he's got Zanele too. That is what he has been doing while you've been thanking him for buying you cigarettes."

Jonas gripped my wrists—his hands surprisingly strong. For a moment, I thought he was going to hurt me. Then his mouth fell open, he dropped his hands, and his cap fell to the floor. "No," he said slowly. "No."

"Get out," I said. "Go back to your baas. Go help him kill your daughters."

Jonas picked up his cap from the floor. He steadied himself against the shop counter. And then he left. I was shaking.

BY THE TIME I GOT ONTO A PUTCO BUS, IT WAS ALREADY afternoon. And a big Coca-Cola truck was in the road, blocking our way to the shebeen. The truck looked new, and had a large close-up of a white girl's freckled face, with the lettering, COKE ADDS LIFE, but I couldn't see what it added life to.

## Zanele

I PUT THE PHONE IN ITS CRADLE JUST AS A BLACK MERCEDES stopped in front of the house.

Jack ran in from the next room with the fat boy. And they stood there, waiting for me to do something.

I stood up, walked over to the line of closets, and got inside one of them, behind coats. The coats smelled of a faraway place.

Jack came to the closet door and stared down at me. His face was tight. In the dim light, I saw the glint of his eyes, the outline of the bones on his face. Was it possible to love something so imperfect as this? He gave me a tense smile before he closed the closet door.

Then, rapping at the front door. Slow footsteps as Jack went to answer it.

# Jack

I PICKED UP THE GUN FROM THE BEDSIDE TABLE WHERE I'D left it next to the bowl of pasta. I put it in my waistband. The knocking continued. I took Ricky's dad's dressing gown and put it on. "Make yourself useful and answer the door."

Ricky just stood there.

I walked down the stairs. And Ricky followed.

I opened the door. A man dressed in an old blue suit. He had a burn on one cheek, light, almost papery textured hair.

He smiled. "Hello. Jack Craven, yes?" His eyes went behind me. "And Richard Kretsky, yes."

I stood there, waiting, with the door open.

"May I come in?" His eyebrows rose with the question, but his eyes remained lazy, expressionless. I thought about taking the gun out and shooting him. Maybe I should have.

I stepped back from the door. "Of course."

He stepped in and the wood creaked. Ricky backed away as the man entered. Ricky must have told him we were here.

"It wasn't Richard, Jack," the man said in his pleasant, measured voice. "Don't worry. Richard just left in such a hurry, and his parents, lovely, really lovely people, told me he'd rushed here. Richard tells his parents the truth. He didn't know I was coming. You can't blame him."

We were standing under an old-fashioned chandelier. The man walked to the living room. He seemed to know his way around the house. I didn't see a gun on him, but then what did I know. "And you are?"

He turned. "How rude of me. Sorry. Coetzee. Michael Coetzee." And he held out his hand, and looked unsurprised when neither of us took it. Then he started walking up the stairs. I followed him. Ricky followed me.

"What do you want?" I said.

"Wouldn't it be better to have this conversation when all

of us are together?" Coetzee said. "I think Zanele would like to be part of it too." He entered the second bedroom and his hand ran over the undisturbed bed. "Where is she?"

The door to the master bedroom was ajar. He knocked on the door and entered. Sunlight through the curtain fell on the bed and picked out the red tint of the wooden floor.

"What a lovely room," he said. He walked around the bed.

I watched him walk past the closet to Ricky's mother's dressing room. His eyes scanned the clothes on the shelves, the perfume in pink bottles. He walked to the door. A turn, and then he was back at the closets. He flung open the first and then the second one, the doors swinging back and hitting the wall with hollow slaps. Ricky jumped at the sound. I took the gun out. Coetzee looked at it and smiled.

"Step away," I said.

Coetzee didn't move.

I undid the safety catch. "That's the catch. It's loaded."

"I believe you," Coetzee said.

Then Ricky slapped the gun out of my hand. It clattered to the floor between Coetzee and me.

"You crazy, Jack?" His voice was shrill. The real Ricky, under all the other Rickys.

I reached for the gun. But Coetzee was there first. He knocked me backward, his knuckles viciously swiping my face. Ricky picked up the gun.

"Ricky," Coetzee said. "Give me the gun."

Ricky was holding it, trembling.

"Give it to me, Ricky," Coetzee repeated.

And Ricky did.

"Sit on the bed. Both of you," Coetzee said, directing us with the barrel of the gun. "That means you, Jack."

The door of the cupboard opened. Zanele put one bare foot on the floor and then the other. My shirt was loose on her. Its tails reached her knees.

# Zanele

I PUSHED OPEN THE CLOSET DOOR. WHEN HE SAW ME, Coetzee's face did not change expression—the gun was pointed at the fat boy and Jack. They were sitting on the bed. I stepped out.

His eyes went back to the boys. And I jumped at him, reaching for the gun. Jack sprang from the bed. A shot went off. Jack fell back. The dressing gown bloomed a darker red over his arm.

Coetzee gripped my neck and pushed me onto a kneeling position. Jack's shirt slid down over my legs like a dress.

"I didn't want to do this," Coetzee said, putting the barrel of the gun against the side of my head. "You didn't give me a choice." He pulled me up, the gun digging into my temple, and forced me onto the bed.

"Everyone sit down," he said.

So we did. The fat boy, Jack, and then me, my arm touching his bleeding one.

"I know there's going to be a special delivery to Swaziland tonight," Coetzee said. "Where is the pickup?" He pushed the gun deeper into my head.

I moved my eyes away from the neat black surface of the gun to Coetzee's face.

"You are not being clever," Coetzee said. "Shame, your father must have the brains in the family. Not many. But some."

"He's dead," Jack said.

"Not yet," Coetzee said. "But soon. I always knew something wasn't right about him. Something passed on to this girl." He moved the barrel of the gun toward Jack. "To the children you might have had, yes?"

He shifted the gun under Jack's chin, sliding it over his throat. "Yes?"

"Yes," Jack answered. His voice was flat. Like he didn't care anymore.

"Jack, let me explain to you. It will be very easy for me to kill her. You understand?"

"I understand," Jack said.

"Good. I will ask again. Where is the pickup?"

My eyes found Jack's.

He cleared his throat. "You see, Mr Coetzee, it's not a case of where."

"I'm running out of patience, my friend," Coetzee said.

"They'll only meet if Zanele sings. You kill her, they won't meet. She's the signal." Jack's voice had gone softer.

My voice rose like I was about to cry. "How could you tell him, Jack?"

"Had to. He was about to blow your head off," Jack said, not looking at me.

Coetzee put the gun against my forehead. "What is this place?"

"Don't you know?" I said. "I'm the best singer in Soweto."

# TWENTY-ONE

## Thabo

MEENA CAME TO THE SHEBEEN AROUND FIVE TO TELL ME. THE two boys were there, and Sunny was smoking a cigarette outside.

"Special Branch," she said.

"Special Branch what?"

"They have Zanele."

This girl had stitched me up many times—but this time she didn't know what to do.

I almost told her that I had told Sam Shenge, who must have told the abo gata. Wasn't I allowed to be angry for a minute, a second? How could I know that news travelled so fast to the other side of Joburg?

All I said was, "Okay."

"Do something," she said.

"What's there to do?"

"You just keep rubbing that glass. It's polished already."

I put the glass down on the counter. With me sitting on a stool, we were eye to eye.

"It's all over, isn't it?" she said.

My head went down. Down until it came onto her bony shoulder. Then she patted my back. Me, I didn't even deserve this. I should have been left out there when Lerato stabbed me.

## Meena

Thabo didn't know what to do after I told him about Zanele.

He sat out at the back of the shebeen and said nothing. He leaned onto my shoulder for maybe half a minute, but then straightened himself.

"Leave me," he said to me, to his sidekicks, to the large man with the scar who said nothing but smoked just outside the door. Stacks of beer were piled high at the back. Trident—the beer from Jack's warehouse. I didn't say anything, not now.

There were more glasses to polish, things to be put back in place, so I went back and did that. Thabo's sidekicks didn't scare me, even the tall scarred one. Thabo hugging me in front of them seemed enough for them to leave me alone.

Papa would probably send people to look for me. It was past five, but I didn't care now.

Mankwe came in around eight, wearing a wig and a red dress that flared at the bottom. She looked past me at the counter.

"Where's Thabo?" she said.

"Out."

"What do you mean, out? We have a big day today. Happy hour."

I smiled but said nothing. She probably thought there was something wrong with me. She walked past the counter. "It was me," I said. She turned. "I was the one who saved you from jail."

She went out the back door. I thought telling her that I had saved her would make me feel better but it didn't. The Special Branch had Zanele, and I couldn't tell her sister. Not now. I cleaned the glasses and passed them over to the bartender, who stacked them on the shelf. Then I wiped the counter. I was still wiping the counter when three men came in.

I had seen one of them before, the first time the black car had come for cigarettes. He was police. Then came the blond man in a dark blue suit. Coetzee.

And then Jack, with a bandaged arm, stained with blood. Behind him, Zanele. Behind her, more policemen. The barman put all the glasses down and put his hands up. Zanele's lips were pressed into a thin, unmoving line. Jack's were too.

I wanted to shout something, to warn Thabo and Mankwe at the back. My mouth opened and closed. I said nothing. Jack, his eyes wandering around the room, finally saw me. Mankwe and Thabo came through the back door, the police holding them. Thabo was swearing, trying to fight them. His red shirt was all crumpled and his bow tie was loose. Then he saw Zanele and he shouted like he'd seen a ghost.

"Zee?"

"*Yebo*, bhuti," she said, but she was looking at Mankwe—a smile spread over her face.

"Be quiet." The policeman behind her hit her with the side of his gun.

Jack flinched.

"Take your stations," Coetzee said. A red flush had spread up his neck. He looked excited in a terrible way. His eyes scanned the place, every corner, every door, every person.

The policemen fanned around the shebeen. There were at least fifteen of them. Some went outside.

Thabo was still smiling at Zanele like she was Father Christmas. I felt invisible.

"If anyone in this room gives warning to the people coming that the police are here, we will shoot her. No questions, no trial. *Klaar?*" the blond man said, looking at Thabo. And then turning to Zanele, "And I will break your pretty boy's face."

No one said anything.

I got up from the stool.

The blond man pointed at me. "You," he said. "Get her dressed." Then he pointed at Zanele.

"Me?" I said. My voice sounded squeaky, scared.

"You."

## Zanele

"NOT IN THAT BOX, THAT BOX," I SAID TO MEENA, JERKING MY head to the left. She opened the other dress box and rifled through the old clothing. Her fingers fumbled as she picked up an old black dress with sequins.

"Not that one, the red one," I said.

Behind us, a large policeman stood with his gun on us. His eyes, behind the gun, between pouches of skin, were grey.

Meena held up the dress. "She needs to change," she said. "Sir, can you please give us some privacy? Please, can you stand on the other side of that curtain?"

The policeman grunted, moved to the other side of the curtain.

As Meena held the dress out for me to slip into, I whispered in her ear, "They're still coming, right?"

She shrugged.

"Tell Thabo to make a plan before my second song." And the dress was on and the policeman came through the curtain and there was no more time to say anything. I pulled the wig onto my bare head, looked at myself in the mirror—and the policeman pulled us away. I thought, at least Mankwe was free.

# Jack

THEY TIED ME BACKSTAGE WITH A POLICEMAN ON ME.

They had told me I would be returned home on bail in the next few hours.

When Zanele would be dead.

It depended on the gangster and Meena now. There was nothing for me to do.

There were three other policemen inside the shebeen, all black. And the rest, I guessed, in unmarked cars on side streets, waiting for the special delivery.

She would try to escape. And I was glad.

It wasn't like I was sacrificing myself. They wouldn't kill me—I was white.

If she didn't escape, she would die.

Through the curtain, I could see more and more people filing in. The gangster was allowed to walk around and act like he was still a big deal around this place.

I doubted he'd been able to put a decent plan in place so quickly. The blood was draining from my head. I felt dizzy, staring at the gangster's hat, flashy, silver, an overt slant to the brim.

"Ah mlungu," he said, coming backstage. "How are you today?"

I nodded.

The gangster smiled, looking down at my bloody arm. Then he took off his hat and put it on my head. The policeman's eyes shifted to the hat, nudged the gun against the tsotsi's back, pushing him away. But what harm could a silver hat do.

IT WAS NINE. ZANELE AND HER SISTER STILL HADN'T COME OUT. The saxophonist started fiddling with a few long notes. The piano player sat on the stool, a thin man with a single drum in front of him.

They eased into the set and people started ordering beer. Then Zanele's sister came on stage.

This was the first time I had seen her. I could tell why the police had made a mistake. They looked alike, but her sister's eyes were bigger, her face more delicate.

"*Sawubona* abantwana," she said, and there was something gentle, magical in her voice. "Today, the first song. *West Wind*. Mama Makeba."

A cheer went up in the house. Zanele was probably somewhere close, waiting. With a gun at her back.

"West wind," her sister breathed into the microphone, the other instruments silent. "Blow ye gentle," then the piano came in, hesitant, like her voice. "For the souls of yesterday . . ." she trailed off, and the audience urged her on. This time her voice came in powerful. "My sons, proud and noble. Here within my heart they lay."

Where was Zanele?

Mankwe sang on. And the audience was reminded of the children who'd died in the riots, as if they needed reminding. Their mood followed her voice rising to a festive anger.

Then a voice joined hers.

The men in the audience parted for Zanele as she joined Mankwe. She walked slowly, holding her arms and her head high. Her voice was loud, almost a shout. The sequins shimmered on her dress as she took her place next to her sister, and the audience whistled and shouted in Zulu.

It still was a miracle to me that she was alive. And now I imagined for a moment—because the blood was leaving my head—that I was sitting here, just having a drink and watching Zanele perform and, you know, we were seeing each other. Legally. With everyone knowing.

I smiled at how ridiculous that was. Then the policeman prodded my wounded arm.

# Thabo

IT WAS ALMOST TEN. MY OLDER BOY, NKOSI, SHOULD HAVE SET off by now from the power station. In half an hour, he would come to pick up Zanele and the others in my car. One of the bush boys was in the shebeen, dressed as a girl. Two others lingered three streets away, waiting for the car.

Now, because of the abo gata, I needed a distraction that would take them off Zanele. Then I needed Zanele in the car before they could shoot her. I had two guns, with maybe two or three bullets each, two boys who would do what I told them. A car. No good that Sunny was tied up in a police car.

No wait, two cars. I still had the Impala I had stolen the day of the protest. It was beat up, but the accelerator worked fine.

A distraction—I needed a distraction.

And then I thought of the mlungu. Everything started to take shape in my mind.

Meena stepped outside. She was wearing the red dress that Zanele used to wear for her solo show. Another time I would have laughed.

"Take this." I handed her my old gun. "Only two bullets. Use them well."

"So what are you going to do?" Meena asked, putting it in her school bag.

"Aye, thula. Let me think."

"Think then," she said. "Just make sure there's room for me."

"What?"

"I'm coming in the car too." She turned to go back inside.

"There is only space for five," I said. "You crazy?"

"Figure it out, tsotsi," she said.

"Ah, you are funny."

"I'm serious."

This whole time, she had been the most reliable, more than

my boys, more than Sunny. Now, when the whole pack of abo gata was on us, she was demanding crazy things.

If my plan worked, I would rule these streets. The whole township would know.

But first, one small thing. I went inside the shebeen, cocked my head. Thulani walked up to me with an empty crate of beer.

"Go to Pillay's All Purpose and give them this message. I don't care if they're closed," I said. "You break their windows if you have to, and make them come here, round the back. The back, you understand." I handed him Meena's school blazer. "Give them this."


# Jack

NOW IT WAS ONLY ZANELE AT THE MICROPHONE. SHE HELD her hand up to get everyone quiet. "*Siyabonga, bafowethu.* Siyabonga. This song," she said, "is a new one for me. I have never sung this song."

A chuckle went through the room.

"Aye," she said. "I know, I will not sing it like Mankwe, but thula wena."

The saxophonist started playing first, a sort of dreamy, almost sad, melody. Once it had faded out, Zanele started to sing. Her eyes went to the front rows, the back rows, and then backstage—to me. I recognized the song. "Summertime." A time when the cotton grew high, the fish were jumping in their lakes. A rich boy, with a rich father and a good-looking mother. He didn't need to worry because he had these things.

"Hush, little baby," Zanele sang to me, her voice soft. "Don't you cry." And she was smiling. Smiling at a time like this.

It was Zanele's goodbye. I wouldn't have expected it from her. She could have gone off with just a glance.

I remember the last time I came here, thinking that the place was tacky, the singer, bad.

Meena ran onstage and pulled Zanele around in a kind of square dance. The pianist obliged, speeding up the tempo.

Yelling from the back of the shebeen. And then there were four, maybe five people running at me, shouting "mlungu." More people. I toppled, still tied. The silver hat came off my head. I tried and tried to pull my hands out of the cuffs. The policeman gripped me by the neck and waved his gun.

But he lost me to the mob. I was dragged along the floor as more and more people came at me.

The policeman shouted into his walkie-talkie. Then shots. My head grazed stones as I was dragged out of the shebeen. More screams. I felt blood spreading over my face, my eyes.

Then I was picked up and thrown onto the back seat of a car. The silver hat was back on my head.

The gangster's face appeared through the window, a smile stretched his face. "You are the distraction, my friend."

He came around the back seat and propped me up. He put a mound of smelly clothes next to me. On top of the mound, he put a woman's black wig.

Then he got in the front of the car and started the engine.

"Where are you taking me?"

"To the police."

"And this wig's meant to be Zanele?"

"Be quiet, mlungu. I didn't see you come up with a plan."

And then behind us, in the dark, headlights. The police.

They were gaining on us.

The gangster swerved onto a narrow street. We lost a car, but the other one was still behind us.

Then they started shooting. Thabo leaned down in his seat and I dropped to my side, away from the mound of clothes. A shot came through the glass. The wig flew off—hit the front windscreen.

The gangster kept driving. He turned right, tires screeching. But a police car waited at the other end, lights flashing.

Policemen on all sides of the car. The gangster raised his hands.

"Good try," I said.

He didn't reply.

# TWENTY-TWO

## Meena

As soon as the crowd started after Jack, Thabo's older boy cut the lights. More screaming. I pulled Zanele off-stage—out through the side entrance where the car was waiting.

And behind us, the police. "Everyone stop. Hands up," the blond one said. The same one I'd seen before in the shop. Zanele put her hands up slowly, the boy in the driver's seat got out and put his hands up too. So did the two boys and the woman. Behind the policeman were stacks and stacks of Jack's father's beer.

I pulled the trigger. I missed the policeman. The bullet hit the beer. Then again. A crate toppled, shards of glass everywhere.

I threw myself at the open door of the car—Zanele was already inside. Thabo's boy hit the accelerator with the doors still open, the woman dragged herself inside. The other two hung on to the doors of the car. More shots. One was pulled off. The other let go. They fell onto the road.

The black Mercedes, the blond man's car, was behind us. There was no sign of the boys now, only the dim outline of the Mercedes in the dark.

## Thabo

THEY PUT US IN THE BACK SEAT, ME NEXT TO THE MLUNGU. Then they tied our hands together. The mlungu's blood was on my suit, my face. He was dirty and smelly. He was smiling, and kept muttering stupid things to me, like how I was a "good one."

"Thula wena," I said to him.

The mlungu closed his eyes and leaned on my shoulder. I pushed him off. His head came down again.

After all their conversation about going here, going there in Afrikaans, the abo gata started the car. We were heading for the highway, not the station.

I DIDN'T SEE THE COCA-COLA TRUCK UNTIL IT HIT THE BLACK Mercedes. The Mercedes flew off the highway, down, down, until it crashed on the road below. The truck just stayed there in the middle of the highway, blocking two lanes.

From the sky, God had dropped a crazy Coca-Cola truck driver. Now maybe I would go to church.

One of the policemen got out of our car to check what had happened. There was only one abo gata left in the car.

I looked over at the mlungu. He was awake, staring at the truck.

The mlungu jerked when he heard the shot, and then his mouth opened—opened when he looked at where the abo gata had been. Because he had been shot in the head and his head had hit the window. I stared at the shattered glass. Then I saw in a small boy's hand, a gun. My gun. In a car I recognized. Thulani.

The boy was smiling like he had won a Mr Soweto beauty contest. "Hurry, hurry, Thabo—"

Up ahead, in the noise and smoke, the abo gata hadn't noticed. Yet.

Thulani got out of the Impala, ran out, reached through the shattered window and opened the door.

"Get the key."

"What key?"

"Ai wena, the one for these handcuffs. His pocket."

The boy pulled us out, tied together, onto the road, the mlungu leaning on me. We rolled into the Impala. Shouts in Afrikaans, but Thulani didn't need to be told, he was in the driver's seat, turning, and we were driving through the broken divider to the other side, leaving the Coca-Cola truck, all those dead abo gata behind. I trained my boys well.

"Take the next exit," the mlungu said, leaning back, like we were his drivers picking him up from the Carlton Hotel. He looked sick. "Take us to say bye."

"Be quiet, mlungu," I said. "Try staying alive."

## Jack

THERE WAS A MOMENT WHEN I THOUGHT THE CAR WOULDN'T fall. But then a piece of the metal barrier broke off and everything stopped bending. The Mercedes flipped and spun before it fell. And then a fire, taking over the sky.

The front of the Coca-Cola truck was smashed in. The advertising on its side was untouched—a girl with a Coca-Cola bottle and the words: COKE ADDS LIFE.

THE BOY DROVE US OFF THE HIGHWAY AND THEN TURNED US back toward the border. He took us through lonely rural back roads, empty roads, through flat yellowed land and stunted trees. It seemed like a long time before he stopped.

•   •   •

When I woke up, there were two cars facing each other and figures against the lightening sky, arguing. Meena's father with his arms around her. Meena was screaming.

And there was Zanele, standing a little to the side. Alive.

The tsotsi got out of the car like he had expected all this to happen, his face bloody. They all ran to him with questions. Zanele ran to him and he lifted her up shouting, happy. Her head was flung back and he was looking up at her.

Last goodbyes. The boy driving our car scrambled into Zanele's car.

And then, finally Zanele saw me and came to my car. She put her fingers over the cuts on my face. "They will pay for this."

"Is that all you have to say?"

"For now, yes." Still her touch on my face, and it was unbearably painful, all of it.

"Help me out," I said.

"We don't have much time."

"I just want to stand up."

I held on to her and we walked over to the others. Meena, still screaming, was being pulled by her father.

I sat down in Zanele's car. Then she got in.

"You're not thinking straight," she said. She was scared, her eyes gave her away. Scared that I didn't really mean it.

That was enough for me.

Then we were driving away, waving—me with my good arm and she with both of hers—at the lonely figure of the gangster against the battered car. And then, we were speeding in the pitch black—and my eyes closed. I leaned into Zanele against the itchy texture of her sequined dress.

In front of my eyes, my mother went by, Ricky, Joubert, Coetzee. My house, and then the intricate, rolling spires of Oxford.

# TWENTY-THREE

## Meena

I LEARNED LATER THAT IT HAPPENED LIKE THIS. JONAS WENT
home after I told him that Coetzee had been hunting his
daughters. What I know from the newspaper reports is that
Jonas took his baas's gun from its locked drawer and hijacked
a Coca-Cola truck. *The Rand Daily Mail* said that specialists
had found a tumour growing in his brain.

I'd like to think that Jonas got to see his daughters singing
in the shebeen. Maybe he thought about how Mankwe must
have got her voice from him, and Zanele maybe his smile.
Maybe, at the last moment, he regretted leaving them.

What we do know is that he followed Coetzee and the rest
of us out of Soweto. Jonas knew his roads, knew his highways
in and out of Johannesburg. He had taken trains in and out,
buses, driven a black Mercedes, all his life. And finally—dead
in a Coca-Cola truck.

Zanele wouldn't know what her father did for her.

One day I will tell her.

## Thabo

NO ONE GOES TO PILLAY'S ALL PURPOSE TO ASK FOR MONEY
now, not even the other gangs. They know Pillay knows me,
and everyone in Soweto knows that I made twenty abo gata
disappear last month. A few tsotsi? Easy. Now all the boys who
are afraid of going to jail beg me to get them across the border.

Desperate people find money somehow.

Yes, the police are after me, but they are after a lot of people these days. More and more of us leave for the borders, and protests across the country.

Maybe I will start my own gang. Sizwe knows I am thinking about doing this, but he says nothing. I am powerful now. They all know he tried to get me killed, and I came back from the dead.

I think of Zanele often, especially at night when the shebeen is closed and it is just Mankwe and me.

We talk about her, but it's never enough.

It is hard for Mankwe, because she has to earn for both of them. I help out a bit. Mama Lillian stays in the house now and speaks even less than before.

I think of the last time I saw Zanele, how I had lifted her up, and how happy she was to see me. She had said, "I need to check on him." And she went right past me to the Impala with the sick mlungu in the back.

I think of the way Zanele held her bleeding mlungu the last time I saw them.

I said, "Take your broken bird. He probably won't make it."

I get less and less angry about it as days go by. That's what I tell myself.

I come to the shop often because Meena is the only one who knows what happened. But she won't talk to me. Not last month, not last week, not tomorrow.

One time she did leave something for me. On the counter, she left the *Sunday Times* newspaper open at the page about Zanele's father being the man who drove the Coca-Cola truck.

So I keep coming. Her father says Meena is going to medical school next year. Somehow her exam marks were good enough, he says, and shakes his head. Now she just has to make sure her December exams go okay.

He offers me free things. Old Spice. "Very nice. Imported."

Most times I say no. Sometimes I say yes.

I think of Meena as a proper doctor in a big hospital like Baragwanath. Agh, maybe in ten years I will be the same as I am now, but rich. We will meet at an operating table, and she will be pulling bullets out of me, and I will say, ai wena, I know you. I don't trust you with a knife.

# Meena

I STILL READ NEWSPAPERS. I'M STILL ALLOWED TO DO THAT. Mostly I read old papers, starting from June. Then I read through all the stories, to Jonas. A week later, an obituary for Jack Craven, a picture of him in his rugby uniform, a cup in hands. No mention that he was still technically missing, that he ran off with a black girl across the border. This was, probably, a tidier ending for his parents.

Most of the time, I have to stay in my room and study. That is all Papa says. Once or twice, he tried to talk about other things, ask me questions, talk about when Mami died, but what's the point? Maybe for him this story starts there, but not for me.

If Thabo hadn't told Papa, I wouldn't be here, but in Swaziland with Zanele and the rest. Training.

I remember the way he just stood there as Papa took me away.

My grandmother comes in every few hours, with more cooked food. She thinks if she makes me enough food, I will be happy again, that everyone will go back to how they were. Maybe this was how it was when Papa came back from jail all those years ago.

Sometimes it's Jyoti who brings the food to my room. She likes to sit in my lap and say nothing, so I let her. One time last week, she came to my room with a chocolate truffle. She didn't know what it was, but she handed it to me and said it was from Fancy Man. And when I didn't want it, she was happy to eat it herself. On the inside of the wrapper, there were three words: You Belong Here.

Just the type of thing he would do.

He doesn't need to come to the store; he just comes because he likes Papa being grateful to him. It's horrible. I imagine that he's very proud of what he did, getting Zanele, Jack, and that other boy across the border. I bet he forgets to mention the Coca-Cola truck in the story. And the truck was there only because I told Jonas.

I wonder what Zanele and Jack are doing. I imagine them walking down a street together. There is something careless about the way they walk, past houses and their staring owners, past shop fronts dull in the morning light.

They're an attractive couple, too attractive—shining a little too bright.

One day I'll get a postcard with a short message: "We're OK." Or something like that.

I wait for it.

# HISTORICAL NOTE

On June 16, 1976, a shot rang out—a bullet from a policeman's gun that found its way to Hastings Ndlovu, a high school student in Soweto, Johannesburg, South Africa. Hastings was 15. In all, around 200 students were believed to have died that day, a day which would be later known as the Soweto Uprising. Hastings Ndlovu and Hector Pieterson were two of the first victims.

Earlier, in the morning of June 16, more than fifteen thousand students, from schools around the township, met up according to a pre-planned route and organized themselves into a march to the Orlando Stadium to protest against the BANTU EDUCATION ACT, or "Baas Law." Sources from the time indicate that the police hadn't been prepared for this protest, nor were most of the students' parents.

To understand why a policeman was given the power to shoot at unarmed black students, we have to go months, years, decades back. In 1976, most teenagers had been born into the system of apartheid, a racial policy in South Africa that made it legal to racially discriminate against non-white people. Non-whites were denied equal rights to decide where they lived, where they could work, where they were permitted to shop, and what type of education they could receive, among many other restrictions. Apartheid was written into law in 1948.

Students realized that the new education law for blacks, the Baas Law, would make it extremely difficult to complete their education, in a schooling system that already had too few books, too few teachers, too few schools. Students had been learning most of their subjects in English, already a second language, for most of their lives. Now, students in Grade 10 or below would be forced, in a matter of weeks, to switch to learning in Afrikaans, the dominant language of the ruling National Party.

Students in 1976 had lived with the stories of their parents' and their grandparents' experience of apartheid. All major political movements were banned, and many of the leaders of parties that opposed apartheid, like Nelson Mandela, were in prison. The students' parents and their grandparents had seen the consequences of opposing the government—life imprisonment, sometimes death.

Students in 1976 realized they couldn't wait for their political leaders to be set free.

Now it was their time to act.

# GLOSSARY

**Abantwana:** *noun, Zulu.*
Children.
Note singular "umtwana" as below.

**Abo gata:** *slang, noun, plural, Zulu.*
Police.

**Afrikaans:**
A language of southern Africa, derived from the form of Dutch
brought to the Cape by Protestant settlers in the 17th century.
Could also refer to this group of people.

**Amandla:** *noun, Zulu.*
Strength, power, force, might.

**ANC:**
The African National Conference. Formed in 1912, the organization
led efforts to protest against discriminatory legislation. The
organization was banned in 1960, but continued significant
underground activity through the 1970s.

**Asibe sabe thina:** *song, Zulu.*
We Shall Not Fear.

**Asseblief:** *interjection, Afrikaans.*
Please.

**Baas:** *noun, Afrikaans.*
Boss, master.

**Baba:** *noun, Zulu, from ubaba.*
Father, dad.

**Bafowethu:** *noun plural, Zulu from Abafowethu.*
My/our brothers.

**Baie:** *adverb/adjective, Afrikaans.*
Very much.
Note: Baie dankie means "thank you very much."

**Bhuti:** *noun, Zulu, from ubhuti.*
Brother.

**Boer:** *noun, English.*
A South African of Dutch extraction/origin. Commonly used to reference Afrikaans people.

**Braai:** *noun, Afrikaans and English.*
Barbecue.

**Bru:** *slang, English and Afrikaans.*
Shortened from Afrikaans boer, meaning "brother."

**Clever:** *noun, slang.*
Clevers are 'streetwise city-slickers,' and may also be gangsters, but non-gangsters may aspire to the style, (Glaser, 2000). From E. Hurst. *Tsotsitaal, global culture and local style: identity and recontextualisation in twenty-first century South African townships.*

**Dagga:** *noun, South African, informal.*
Marijuana.

**Dankie:** *verb, interjection, Afrikaans.*
Thank you.

**Domkop:** *noun, Afrikaans.*
Dummy.

**Eish:** *noun, Zulu.*
An exclamation expressive of surprise, agreement, disapproval, etc.

**Gaan blaas:** *insult, Afrikaans, literal definition.*
Go blow yourself up.

**Gogo:** *noun, Zulu, from ugogo.*
Grandmother.

**Highveld:** *noun, English.*
Plateau land with an elevation of about 4,000 feet used especially for grazing. Partial translation from Afrikaans hoogveld, from hoog (high) and veldt (field).

**Ja:** *interjection, Afrikaans.*
Yes.

**Jol:** *verb, slang, South African.*
To party, have fun.

**Kak:** *Afrikaans.*
Bird droppings, shit.

**Kaffir:** *noun, offensive racial term.*
An insulting term for a black African person in South Africa.

**Kahle:** *interjection, Zulu.*
Wait.

**Klaar:** *verb, Afrikaans.*
Finished, clear.

**Klap:** *verb, noun, Afrikaans.*
Hit, strike.

**Koeksister:** *noun, Afrikaans and English.*
Afrikaans dessert, braid-shaped doughnut, infused with syrup.

**Koppies:** *noun, English, from Afrikaans.*
Small hills in a generally flat area.

**Masibulele ku Jesu, ngokuba wasifela:** *Hymn, Zulu.*
Let us thank Jesus, for He died for us.

**Mealie:** *noun, English.*
Corn.

**Meneer:** *noun, Afrikaans.*
Mister.

**Mfana(s)/Bafana(pl):** *noun, Zulu.*
Singular mfana from umfana, boy. Plural bafana from abafana, boys.

**Mlungu:** *noun, Zulu, from umlungu.*
White person.

**Moer:** *slang, verb, noun.*
To attack (someone or something) violently.

**Nkosi S'ikelele:** *song, Zulu, Xhosa, and other.*
Title of South African's national anthem, from 1994 to present. The literal translation, from Xhosa, is "God Bless Africa." Nkosi Sekelel' iAfrika was originally composed in 1897 by Enoch Sontonga, a Methodist school teacher. The song started being sung as a church hymn but later was sung as part of political protest against the apartheid government in South Africa.

**Oke:** *slang, South African.*
Word for a person, usually male.

**Paap:** *noun, Afrikaans, English.*
Maize porridge.

**PAC:**
Pan Africanist Congress. South African political party, originally part of the ANC. This party followed an Africanist ideological stance. Further information at: South African History Online: http://www.sahistory.org.za/topic/pan-africanist-congress-pac.

**Putco:**
South African bus company.

**SASM:**
South African Student Movement. An organisation of high school students that represented students, that among other activities, organized boycotts against the Bantu Education. Further information at: South African History Online: http://www.sahistory.org.za/topic/pan-africanist-congress-pac.

**SASO:**
South African Students Organisation. An organisation focused on Black Consciousness. Its inaugural president was Steve Biko. Further information at: South African History Online: http://www.sahistory.org.za/topic/pan-africanist-congress-pac.

**Sawubona:** *interjection/greeting, Zulu.*
Hello, Good Morning/Afternoon/Evening.

**Shebeen:** *noun, English.*
South African name for an illegal bar, typically located in a township.

**Sisi:** *noun, Zulu, from usisi.*
Sister.

**Siyabonga:** *verb/greeting, Zulu.*
He/She/We thank you.

**Suka:** *verb, Zulu.*
Go away, go off.

**Tata Madiba:**
Name for Nelson Mandela. Tata is a Xhosa word for father, while Madiba was Nelson Mandela's clan name.

**Thula:** *verb, Zulu.*
Be quiet, be silent, be still, be peaceful, be tranquil, shut up.
Note: Thula wena as used in the book, refers to the imperative and is literally translated as "you, be quiet."

**Tsotsi:** *noun, English.*
A black street thug or gang member.

**Umkhonto We Sizwe:** *Zulu.*
Literal meaning: Spear of the Nation. This was the name of the armed wing of the ANC. Further information at: South African History Online: http://www.sahistory.org.za/topic/pan-africanist-congress-pac.

**Umntwana:** *noun, Zulu.*
Child.

**Umqombothi:** *noun, Zulu.*
Traditional beer.

**Veld:** *noun, Zulu.*
An area of grassy land with few trees or shrubs especially in southern Africa.

**Voetsek:** *interjection, Afrikaans.*
Get lost.

**Wena** *pronoun, Zulu.*
You.

**Yebo:** *adverb, affirmative interjection, Zulu.*
Yes.

**Zulu:**
The Bantu language of the Zulu people of South Africa. Could also refer to this group of people.

# GLOSSARY SOURCES

*Collins Dictionary*,
http://www.collinsdictionary.com/dictionary/english/.

Dictionary.com,
http://dictionary.reference.com/browse/tsotsi

E. Hurst, *Tsotsitaal, global culture and local style: identity and recontextualisation in twenty-first century South African townships*, (2009). Routledge, Taylor and Francis. http://www.tandfonline.com/doi/pdf/10.1080/02533950903076196.

Glosbe.com, https://glosbe.com/af/en/.

Isizulu net, https://isizulu.net/

Majstro translation website: http://www.majstro.com/Web/Majstro/bdict.php?gebrTaal=eng&bronTaal=afr&doelTaal=eng&teVertalen.

*Merriam Webster Dictionary*,
http://www.merriam-webster.com/dictionary/.

*Oxford Dictionary*,
http://www.oxforddictionaries.com/definition/english/.

South African History Online, http://www.sahistory.org.za/topic/.

The Presidency, South African,
http://www.thepresidency.gov.za/pebble.asp?relid=265.